the ones you do

# the ones you do

## Daniel Woodrell

Henry Holt and Company
New York

Published by Henry Holt and Company, Inc.,
115 West 18th Street, New York, New York 10011.
Published in Canada by Fitzhenry & Whiteside Limited,
91 Granton Drive, Richmond Hill, Ontario L4B 2N5.

Library of Congress Cataloging-in-Publication Data
Woodrell, Daniel.
The ones you do / Daniel Woodrell.
p.      cm.
I. Title.
PS3573.06263054 1992
813'.54—dc20
ISBN 0-8050-0972-8

Henry Holt books are available at special discounts
for bulk purchases for sales promotions, premiums,
fund-raising, or educational use. Special editions
or book excerpts can also be created to specification.
For details contact: Special Sales Director,
Henry Holt and Company, Inc., 115 West 18th Street, New York, New York 10011

First Edition—1992

Book Design by Claire Naylon Vaccaro
Printed in the United States of America
Recognizing the importance of preserving
the written word, Henry Holt and Company, Inc.,
by policy, prints all of its first editions
on acid-free paper. ⊗
1  3  5  7  9  10  8  6  4  2

FOR KATIE AND LEIGH

*"If it weren't for the rocks in its bed,
the stream would have no song."*

—*Carl Perkins*

# part i

## Criminentlies

(cry-men-ent-lees)

# 1.

After his wife stole the gangster's money and split on him, she wanted to rub his nose in her deed, so she sent him a note. John X. Shade was sitting on a stool behind the bar in the main room of Enoch's Ribs and Lounge, his gray head bowed, his lean shaky fingers massaging his temples. The safe gaped open and empty behind him, and a bottle of Maker's Mark, sour mash salvation, sat sealed and full on the bar top before him.

The note that was meant to make him feel pitiful as well as endangered was delivered by his ten-year-old daughter, Etta. She came in the side door and through the sea shell and driftwood decor of the lounge where her mother had been the musical entertainment before taking up thievery, carrying a small pink vinyl suitcase that had a picture of Joan Jett embossed on the lid. The girl had thick black hair cut in a fashion her mother, Randi Tripp, considered hip, this being a feminine sort of flattop with long rat-tail tresses dangling down the back of her neck. She wore a green T-shirt that was pro-manatee and rag- gedy jeans that were hacked off just below the knees. A black plastic crucifix hung lightly from her right ear. Her actual name was Rosetta Tripp Shade, but she preferred to be called Etta.

"Mail call," she said and tossed the envelope onto the bar beneath John X.'s chin. She climbed up onto a stool across the rail. "She said you should read it pronto."

Enoch's wasn't a popular spot until late at night when last-call Lotharios from along the Redneck Riviera would fill it up, rooting around after pert and democratic Yankee tourists whose off-season dream vacations had yet to be consummated. It was not open at all this early in the day, so the two were alone. Hot Gulf Coast sun beat in through the smoked windows, warming the joint. On the walls there were community bulletins announcing upcoming fish frys, Gospel shows, ten-K runs for various Mobile charities, and several large, glamorous glossies of Randi Tripp, the 'Bama Butterfly.

John X. started to rip the envelope, then saw the sweat on his daughter's face and felt a trickle stream down his own temples. He shoved the shiny beverage cooler open and said, "I ain't King Farouk, kid, but I'll spot you a bottle of RC."

Etta grinned and grabbed the cold bottle of Royal Crown Cola that he slid to her.

"Well, I ain't Madonna, neither," she said, "but I could drink one."

He opened the envelope and unfolded the letter. It was

on yellow paper scented with lilac, and he spread it flat on
the bar to read.

John X. (no dear for you),
  You are not a clean fit with my future. I have
made a choice and it was in favor of following
my dream as you by now know. I leave special
Etta with you on account of my dreams, for it is
a lonely road I must travel to the top. Here I am
always Enoch Tripp's daughter and many say
that's why I am always featured singer here. I
have talent! My voice fills a room to capacity with
any advertizing at all. Motherhood is one thing
but what is that compared to the many gifts of
song! You know this too. The money I have borrowed for good to invest in my dreams was only
a killer's loot. What good fine thing would he
ever do with it? Europe loves ballads of amore
and shitty luck and am I ever the thrush for them!
I realize Lunch will think the money is still his
but having it is nine-tenths of the law and all of
spending it. You have a silver tongue, shine it up
and maybe Lunch will believe your tale of inno-
cence. Many is the time I have. Enoch is on those
sad last legs and I have told him ciao.
                                        Randi


P.S. I have a sense of my own destiny now. My
sense of my own destiny is that you're not anywhere in it. I was young and married old, a classic story. But Etta will fit in with me down the
road—I'll have my Lear jet fetch her to me where

the nights are sweeter than sweet and full of music and could be she'll like it like me someday.

John X. wadded the letter into a ball and pitched it
at a photo of the 'Bama Butterfly. Great lakes were being
formed on his white shirt by flop sweat.

"Did I have this comin'?" he asked.

Etta retrieved the letter, then lit a match and set it
afire. She dropped the flaming ball into an ashtray, and
watched the flame rise before returning to her stool.

John X. looked at her sadly, then raised the bottle,
cracked the red wax seal, and filled a juice glass with
whisky.

"Criminentlies," he said, "but your ma is some gal,
kid."

"I reckon," Etta said. "She put me off at Shivers Street
and told me to walk here. That gives her time to get gone,
huh, Dad?" She held the soda bottle with both hands, her
body hunched over the bar, eyes down, like a precociously
forlorn honky-tonker. Cosmetics were not foreign to her
young face, and turquoise was the lip color of the day.
"Mom let me pack first, at the trailer."

"What a gal," John X. said.

He pulled the tumbler of whisky close and Etta
watched the glass, then said, "She predicted you'd do that."

"Do what?"

"Pour a giant whisky and have at it."

"Oh," he said. "That didn't call for no crystal ball."
He raised the glass and put the bourbon down in one constant swallow. "And after a drink what'm I goin' to do?"

"She figured we'd go runnin' to the hospital'n see
Grampa Enoch."

As he poured himself another dollop John X. nodded and said, "Then what?"

"Well, she wasn't sure for sure, but her best guess was, flee. She figured we'd flee."

Lunch Pumphrey was called Lunch because if he had a chance to he'd eat yours for you. The stolen money had originally been won down at Hialeah on a horse named Smile Please by two hunch-playing dentists from Baltimore and then tushhogged from them in The Flamingo Motel by Lunch, the thirtyish badass who was a silent partner in Enoch's Ribs and Lounge. Lunch was a loud partner in a bunch of nasty this-and-that along the Gulf Coast between Biloxi and Tampa, but his home port was here in Mobile. It was said of him that he hurt people over business, or pleasure, depending on opportunity, and that his services as a pistolero were in some demand in distant parts of the nation where his face rang no bells. The loot Lunch had taken from the two hunch-playing dentists who'd briefly considered themselves lucky had been invested in the national pastime and doubled when the Cubs eked one out over Doc and the Mets, then doubled again when the Cubbies beat the Cards two straight. The money had spawned to the amount of forty-seven thousand dollars and was stored in the safe. Yesterday the word got around the lounge that as the season wound down all forty-seven K had been put behind the Cubs, the cable team of Lunch's heart, and lost when the Atlanta Braves found some miracle broom and swept them three straight at Wrigley. Lunch had gotten this stunning series of losing bets down with Short Paul of Tampa, who was allegedly wired up asshole to belly button with Angelo Travelina, kingpin of the dangerous dudes in sunkissed country and an aggres-

7

sive debt collector. When Lunch came in today for the cash
to pay off Short Paul and found an empty safe, he could
well decide that both business *and* pleasure dictated that he
hurt a few folks in some marvelously painful manner.

"Criminentlies," John X. said with a groan. He pulled
a cigarette pack from the heart pocket of his shirt and lit
one of the fifty or sixty Chesterfield Kings he inhaled daily.
He lit the smoke with a gray flip-top Zippo lighter that
had the outline of an eight ball etched into it. After exhaling, he said, "I'm not *whelmed* by this, kid. Don't think
I am."

"Dad, I don't think you're whelmed."

"Kid, I refuse to be *whelmed* by this." John X. Shade
had long believed that the key to life was cue ball control,
but lately his stroke was so imperfect on cue balls and life
alike that his existence had come to seem far too much like
the stark moral to a cautionary homily he'd chosen to ig-
nore. He was in his sixties, a decade of his life that suddenly had more miscues and comeuppances in it than he
could construe as merely accidental. His hair was wavy
and thick and partly gray but leaning more and more to
pure white. The physical aspects of his life had taken wicked turns over the last few years, and now his blue eyes had
weakened to the point where they watered over if he stared
at an object ball for more than five seconds, a pitiful de-
velopment for a career billiardist. He also had complaints
from his liver, a creaky left knee, fallen arches, gummy
sinuses, and, to finish off the organic revolt, his hands trembled almost constantly. The trembling hands meant he had
to shakily swat at the cue ball in less than the five seconds
it took his eyes to water over. This series of afflictions had
led to his being victimized by other career billiardists down
to the last copper cent, and thus to his becoming a bar-

tender slash son-in-law mooch six nights a week in Enoch's
Ribs and Lounge.

"Oh, kid," he said, "it's bum luck you're stuck in this
mess with me."

With her thonged feet on the rung of her barstool,
Etta leaned out across the bar and patted the old sport
who was her father on the head.

"You're not totally responsible, Dad."

John X. sat up straight and lifted his chin and stared
into Etta's big 'Bama browns.

"Hell, I know that," he said. He scooted away and
shook open a Winn-Dixie grocery sack. He bent below the
bar to the reserve stock and began to set bottles of booze
into the sack. He showed his loyalty to the Maker's Mark
brand up to four bottles, then impetuously included one
bottle each of gin and rum so that in the weird event he
should want a change from bourbon, he'd have it right
there with him. "People fall out," he said as he lifted the
sack to the counter, "and life rolls on down the road even
after the tread is gone."

Etta jumped from the barstool and went to the wall
by the side door, and there she carefully took down a photo
of her mother. In the photo Randi Tripp was darkly lit and
wreathed in artsy webs of smoke, her eyes cocked in the
manner of a self-aware cutie who had just thrown out an
especially provocative gambit, and her magnificent cleavage and full lips seemed to promise a bounty of luscious
succor for the man with the winning response. Her hair
was black as a crow wing and aloft in a timeless bouffant.

Back at the bar Etta opened her Joan Jett suitcase
and put the photo on top of her clean underthings and the
precious trove of bass lures Grampa Enoch had given her
over the course of several holidays.

John X. reached deep into the floor cabinet for the stiff leather case that held his Balabushka cue, a cue he'd lived with for thirty years, and pulled it out. Dust coated the case, and old pawnshop tags were still stuck to the leather. John X. was studying the tags and the dust when he heard a key going into the front door lock.

"Uh-oh," he said, then spun around and shoved the safe door closed. There was a Budweiser mirror that concealed the safe, but it was on the floor and the front door was opening. John X. looked that way and said, "Hey, Lunch, how're you hangin'?"

" 'Bout a quart too full," Lunch Pumphrey said. His speech was hardy and roughly stylized, with a tangle of Appalachian underbrush in it. He was about five and a half feet of condensed malevolence, wearing a snap-brim hat of black straw, black half-boots, black pants, and one of the long-sleeved black shirts he favored in any weather because they covered the mess of ridiculous tattoos he doodled on his arms when drunk. "Why for's the safe uncovered, Paw-Paw?"

As Lunch came around the bar John X. said, "Flyshit, Lunch. Christ, there was flyshit all over the mirror and gals kept lookin' in it and runnin' out of here thinkin' their lips had sprouted chancre sores. Bad for business. I had to wash it."

Lunch paused with one hand on the bar. His skin was pale and clear of worry lines, his face angular and bony, with dark, sepulchral eyes.

"Still hot," he said, then looked at Etta. "Whew! I bet that there dog won't hunt."

"She don't want to hunt, Lunch," John X. said.

"Just teasin' the child," Lunch said. "My sis used to always pick on me by callin' me bad things, up 'til one day when she stopped callin' me anything at all. What she done was good for me, really, over the long haul." Lunch fanned his face with his hat, then set the hat on the bar. "I got to get somethin' from the safe, Paw-Paw, so back away from there."

John X. looked at Etta, then looked at the whisky bottle on the bar, then looked at the tiny bald spot amid Lunch's burr-cut red hair as Lunch bent to the safe.

"Tonight ought to be quiet here," John X. said as Lunch twirled the combination. Then he grabbed the Maker's Mark bottle with his right hand and smacked it briskly against Lunch's jaw from behind, just below the ear.

Etta screamed as Lunch sagged sideways, his hands clutching at the bottles behind the bar, sending them tumbling to the floor.

The air was soaked with scent from the shattered liquor bottles and Lunch was on all fours, grunting in the eighty-six-proof mire.

"Be human, for cryin' out loud," John X. said, then stepped up and smacked Lunch again. Lunch went out this time, and landed on his chin. John X. spun to face Etta.

Etta's hands squeezed the RC bottle, her eyes shocked circles.

"Get your stuff," John X. said, and she nodded slowly. "We gotta go to the hospital and see if Grampa Enoch knows a way out of this."

He tapped the cash register for the seventy dollars that were in it and added them to the nine bucks in his wallet. Beneath the cash register, on a handy hook, there was a Bulldog .38, and he slipped it off the hook and into a pocket of his light blue shorts. He found a box of shells and took them too. He stuck his pool cue into the sack of liquor and hoisted the load. He came around the bar, opened the front door, and checked the parking lot.

"I hope to God Enoch has some magic in his pocket. Let's get our heinies hoofin' over there and see, huh?"

"I don't have any idea where she run to," Enoch Tripp said. Enoch was a widower, father, father-in-law, grampa, and scoundrel, but he'd been whittled down to a moot point by cancer. His face was bearded, his white hair was matted, and, low in weight as he was, his eyes seemed huge in his thin face. A Bible was clutched in his hands for the first time since Iwo Jima. "Far away I hope."

John X. stood by the window looking out over other wings of the hospital to Mobile Bay. He had a cigarette going.

"We can rule out Europe, I'm pretty damned sure of that," he said.

"She ain't but twenty-eight," Enoch said in a weak voice. "It's good she caught a break."

Etta sat on a chair, pink suitcase on her lap. She had a problem looking straight at Grampa Enoch, who'd taught her many things about the largemouth, the spotted, the red-eye, and even the Suwannee basses, back when he'd been seventy or eighty pounds more alive.

"This is a hell of a note at my age," John X. said. He was rubbing his chin, gazing out at the Bay, watching the regular afternoon rains blow in from the Gulf. Clouds were dark and bunched together, rolling toward land. "Criminentlies, Enoch, I'm two years older'n *you*. Let *that* sink in."

"It is," Enoch said. "It's *all* sinkin' in, Johnny. Every goddamn thing is sinkin' in." He paused to take two deep snuffling breaths. "But Randi could go off and make the Tripp name mean somethin' to the world. Think on that like a dyin' man, would you?" Enoch raised his head from the bed, the weight wobbling atop his weak neck. "Save Etta, Johnny. She's the good thing I've known lately. She's got to where she can cast 'tween twin lily pads, perfect." His head flopped back on the white pillow like a carp tossed on the bank to die. "You got a lot of moves, John X., dust 'em off'n save her."

"Now how can I save us?" John X. asked in a tone of lilting frenzy. He gestured at his feet where there were black low-top sneakers, then his knobby knees and no longer athletic thighs that were visible beneath blue golfer shorts. He plucked a smoke from his heart pocket and lit it with the butt he still had burning. "This's all the clothes I've got. Randi took the car and I've got under a hundred bucks, *E-noch. Buddy.*"

Enoch propped his left elbow on the bed and levered his hand upright. He aimed a finger bone at the closet.

"Take my suitcase. It's got clothes. The truck keys are in this drawer here." His hand fell. "My gift, and welcome to it."

John X. retrieved the suitcase and the truck keys. He could feel the pistol sagging his shorts, and cigarette smoke rose from between his fingers.

"Later on, Enoch."

"Uh," Enoch grunted. "You were my best pal, Johnny, and I couldn't make her *not* do it, so that's that. Randi's blood, and I can't rat out blood."

John X. shrugged and, with down-home grace, waved his cigarette in a gesture of dismissal.

"Aw, forget about it," he said. "Que sera and so on, you know."

Enoch's eyes closed and he said, "See you at the back table on Cloud Nine, Johnny."

"Sure 'nough," John X. said. "I'll stick the balls right up your ass there, too."

"That's good. You always did do that."

John X. gestured at Etta to kiss Enoch good-bye.

"On the cheek?" she whispered.

John X. nodded, then watched her plant one on Enoch's beard. Then she hugged his sick, weary head, but it seemed he didn't care to notice.

As they went down the brightly polished floor of the hallway they did not speak. On the elevator Etta asked, "Why'd she leave, Dad?"

"Well, kid, I always was more Spanky, you see," he said philosophically, "and she was more Alfalfa in type, and that mix ain't good forever."

"Huh," Etta grunted. "She said she outgrew you."

"That's incomplete."

They walked through the lobby and stepped out to the street just as the first fat drops of rain began to fall. Trees shimmied in the Gulf breeze. The streets gave off that nice hopeful smell of fresh rain on hot pavement.

"What's our stragedy, Dad?" Etta asked, using a coined word that was a favorite of his.

He shrugged, then smiled, and his face was briefly as handsome as it had ever been: blue fuck-me eyes, strong chin, proud nose, terrific come hither grin.

"First, find the truck," he said. "Second, flee."

The truck was orange and in sorry condition. The color was owed to a half-price paint sale and the condition to simple neglect. The pistons sounded like a family squabble. A fist-sized gap had developed in the rusted muffler so that exhaust rose into the cab at stoplights. The windshield on the passenger side was webbed with cracks surrounding a .22-caliber hole that resulted from a night when Enoch had taken his coonhounds on a moonlit run across property he'd been warned to stay clear of. The tires were iffy, but the radio worked and all the buttons moved the dial to different country stations. On the tailgate there was a big bumper sticker that read, I Don't Give A Damn *HOW* You Did It Up North.

The liquor was in a plastic ice chest that Enoch had left in the truck bed, minus one bottle that rode in the cab. The two suitcases were on the floorboards under Etta's feet.

The truck was now pulled over on the shoulder of a blacktop road that had a view of The Breeze-In Trailer Park. There was a drizzle of rain and sirens filling the air. John X. reached blindly for the bottle, his eyes steady on the twenty-foot flames rising from his trailer.

"I didn't kill him," he said as his hand found the bottle. "Or hurt him much, either, I don't guess. That there's the sort of thing Lunch does whenever there's a chance of it."

Etta's face was pale, her mouth open. She hadn't looked away from the flames since she first saw them. Her arms were wrapped around her shoulders, hugging herself.

John X. poured two fingers of whisky into a bar glass with pink elephants on it that he'd always kept in Enoch's glove box. He swished the whisky around his mouth, then swallowed. The trailer walls had collapsed inward, and as flames destroyed his most recent home John X. closed his eyes to the awful fact and symbolism of the sight.

"Well, kid," he said sadly. "I'm feelin' the call of the open road. Whatta you think?"

Her eyes stayed bugged on the fire, and her tongue flickered over her young painted lips.

"You're drivin'," she said.

Three hours later the afternoon rains petered out and the sunset was pink and promising. After Pascagoula they'd left the big Gulf Highway for a smaller one that cut away from the coast and was flanked by loblolly pines, barbed wire fences, and chicken shacks.

"Fix me up with a tiny angel, angel," John X. said.

"Just a sec," Etta said. She'd been painting her finger-nails out of boredom, and at present her hands hung from the window to dry the purple polish. The wind blew the black crucifix straight back from her ear. In a few seconds her nails were dry enough, and she pulled her hands in and poured him a tiny angel of Maker's Mark in the pink ele-phant glass. When she held the glass toward him she said, "What'll he do if Lunch should find us?"

"Now don't you worry about that," he said as he took the glass from her hand. "That's my department." He drank the whisky and set the glass on the seat. "I don't want you worrying about that." He kept his eyes on the road and straightened up like he meant business. "I realize I'm a little bit askew as a daddy, but, girl, I want you to know, if anyone messes with you or me, why, I'll get P.O.ed pretty good, and, darlin', when I get mad I'm just like *Popeye*."

## 2.

Over in the delta where the Big River flows brown and strong and sluggish sloughs lurk outside its channels, Rene Shade reclined on a blanket in the small backyard of Nicole Webb's place in Frogtown and watched the sky. He was watching the autumnal parade of millions of birds wending south along the Big River flyway. They followed the river from the near and far north, and now they dominated the sky, coming on in lively legions, in wide variety, honking, tweeting, migrating to wherever. The yearly panorama above was wistful but reassuring to Shade, whose own world had flip-flopped when he'd been suspended from the St. Bruno detective squad for ninety days. The charge was insubordination, but the fact was that he'd failed to cap a disarmed suspect who'd killed a cop.

They'd confiscated his gun and badge and something else he couldn't quite name.

This was his eighteenth day on suspension and there was a jelly jar of tequila sour nestled between his legs. Next to him lay a pile of newspapers and on it there rested a freshly cleaned, unregistered, and thoroughly illegal Taurus .38. His blue eyes had been brushed with redness, and a fresh pink scar had been added to the old familiar ones over his brow. He stared up at the avian parade across an afternoon sky colored heartbroken blue, lifted the pistol in one hand, the jelly jar in the other, and said, "You know, I'm very near to bein' normal, but I just can't get over the hump."

"Well, I like you," Nicole said. She was sitting in a chair against the chicken-wire fence that surrounded the yard, reading a book. The scent from honeysuckle withering on the fence wafted about her. Nicole, out of Texas by way of romance and wanderlust, had been going through a psychedelic cowgirl phase, and she was wearing a sleeveless electric blue shirt with a pearl yoke, red boots with black eagles on them, and faded jeans that were worn to a wispy whiteness and fit her rump as aptly as the word nasty. She was tall and lean and olive skinned with long dark hair pulled back into a great, puffy ponytail. Black-framed reading glasses perched on her nose, but otherwise she came across pretty much like a cowgirl who might've ridden the purple range in some pre-Raphaelite's fever dream. "I like you fine, Rene, but then, I'm partial to sociopaths."

"That's a piece of luck," he said. Shade wore only gray track shorts and a demeanor that was both sullen and mystical. On tiptoes he was a six-footer, thick in the shoulders and arms, bodyshot firm at the waist. The archaic angle of his sideburns and the dead-end-kid swoop of his long brown hair raised some upfront doubts about his good citizenship that his face did nothing to allay. His eyes were blue and challenging, and his nose had been dented artlessly meeting those challenges. Mementos of his free-swinging past had been stitched around his face, the most recent scar still pink above his right eye. Despite his scuffed look there was a ragged allure to his features, and a democratically dispensed "up yours, *too*" aspect to his person that certain neighborhoods took a shine to.

"Maybe I'm where I ought to be—off the cops and back home in Frogtown."

Without looking away from her book Nicole said, "Give it a rest, Rene. You're bad mouthin' yourself into something you'll regret."

It was still warm by day this far downriver but leaves were beginning to fall. The weaker leaves quietly retired from limbs, giving up the struggle in ones and twos, coming down in sad wafting swirls. There was an old children's wading pool in the yard and dead leaves floated on top of the rank water. From a nearby neighbor's porch a radio droned with a college football game, and somewhere down the block a nascent biker gunned his engine like the roar was a symphony to all ears. Shade listened to the symphony and thought that maybe he *was* giving in to fruitless introspection. He set his pistol down, had a swallow of his drink, and asked, "What're you readin', anyhow?"

Her eyes stayed intently on the page.

"It's a collection of short stories about what shithills men are," she said. "It's been gettin' *great* reviews."

"I don't doubt it," he said. He dropped a hand to his crotch and hoisted his rigging. "But that won't change certain facts."

Nicole looked at him and smirked, then raised a hand from the book and pulled the buttons on her shirt open, flashing a pert bare breast at him.

"No," she said, "I reckon it won't." She broke off a blade of grass from the ground beside her and used it as a bookmark. With her arms overhead and her legs stuck out, she stretched and sighed. Then she looked at the pistol and said, "Rene, that pistol is gonna be trouble. You're liable to get caught with it somehow."

Shade shrugged.

"I'd a lot rather get caught *with* it than get caught *without* it."

"Alright. I heard you. I'm not goin' to rag on your ass about it."

The traffic on the flyover once again compelled Shade's interest. He'd loved this sight all of his life and certainly he'd seen many of these exact same birds before. They always returned until death, taking the same path toward the same winter place.

Oh, yeah, they came back and back and back.

"Rene," Nicole said, "you're gettin' that strange moody look again."

"Well, color me weird," he said.

"I don't want to color you weird, I want you to pep yourself up." She put the book down. "I know you've got things on your mind this evening, but I want some fun time, and you ain't fun when you've got that strange moody look on you."

On the bed, in twilight, Shade lay on his back and stared out the window, watching birds float down to roost in nearby trees. "In Memory of Elizabeth Reed" was playing on the stereo and Nicole was playing with his body, using tongue and touch to bring his passion up to scratch. She'd coated him with oil, rubbed his back, fetched him a fresh drink, told him his pecker was pretty, and put in many kind words trying to raise his spirits. Now, her dark hair blooming out wild around her like a swamp shrub that might have stickers on its stems, she straddled him, nuzzling her bush to his nominally stiff dick.

She said, "Oh, sweet," and slid down on him.

His thoughts were out the window, roosting in nearby trees. He said, "Only Redwing blackbirds are in the one tree, and only grackles are in the other."

From her position astride him Nicole shoved a palm firmly against his cheek, pushing his head to the side, then pulled loose and rolled quickly off the bed. She grabbed a T-shirt from the dresser and held it in the hand she shook at him when she said, "Look, you son-of-a-bitch, we ain't been together long enough for you to start passin' out *courtesy* fucks! You hear me?"

"What're you yellin' about?"

"Hey," she said, standing there naked with her hair all akimbo and her hands on her hips. "When we fuck I want your mind on *me*, not on some other fuckin' *species*, Rene. For pity's sake, man, I ain't desperate enough to take charity pokes from the likes of you, or anybody else."

"I'm tired," he said. He sat up on the edge of the bed and again his eyes strayed to the window. "I guess that's what it is."

"You've been this way ever since you got suspended."

"What're you sayin'? You sayin' that I'm a lousy lay now, or what?"

"Oh, geez," she said, and the steam went out of her.

She sagged against the dresser. "I don't believe we want to start tossin' those sorts of bombs around, Rene. Or do you?"

He looked down to his feet on the hardwood floor.

"No, I don't suppose," he said. He conjured up a smile. He patted the bed beside himself. "Come on over here and we'll make love nice, Nic. Set yourself down right here."

Nicole picked her jeans up off a chair and said, "So, you want to make love now, huh? Why don't you get on your knees'n crawl over here and *kiss my ass* and we'll *call it* making love."

Then she went into the bathroom.

Undisturbed now, Shade crouched to the window and stared at the trees where every limb and branch held birds that had come to rest for a night during their long instinctive flight to some destination that was mapped in their bones. The trees and birds were in stark silhouette against the fading light of the sky, and the vision was elemental and exhilarating and comforting.

When Nicole came out of the bathroom in her cowgirl garb and a scowl, Shade went in and took a shower. Then, while some blue grievances were stroked from a fiddle and blasted by the stereo, he shaved and dressed in white pants, white shoes, and a short-sleeved black shirt. He combed his wet brown hair straight back to dry.

He went to the bedside table and lifted his jelly jar for a slosh of tequila but found it to be empty except for ice cubes. He then crossed the flood-warped wooden floor to the kitchen, jar in hand, looking for a refill.

The kitchen was small, as befits a shotgun house, with the stove, sink, and fridge on one side of a narrow aisle, and a high cupboard, shelves, and a small table on the other. The floor was aged linoleum and creaked when Shade walked across it to the freezer.

As Shade dropped ice cubes into the glass and reached for the tequila, Nicole sat at the table facing away from him and said, "You know, from teenaged pink on I always did have the desire in me to be a wanton woman, but I needed to go off and find the right lover to show me how."

"Oh, yeah?" he said, pouring tequila over ice.

"Yeah," she said. "But I ended up meeting you, instead."

"Uh-oh," Shade said. He sensed another one of those a-gal's-gotta-do-what-a-gal's-gotta-do fusses coming on, and he chugged at his drink. But he said, "Your feet ain't nailed to the floor, sister."

She said, "Thinks you."

"Thinks me?" He stared at the back of her head and the olive skin of her slender neck. "Come on, Nic, why don't you roll a couple of joints and listen to the head-phones or something?"

"I can't," she said.

"You can't?"

"Not in my condition."

Slouched against the wall, Shade held the jelly jar with both hands in front of his chest and said, "What condition is that?"

Nicole turned, then stood and faced him. She had a lean, muscular, girl-hoopster body, and eyes of a sea green hue that gave an impression of vastness.

"Well, now," she said, "my condition is I'm pregnant."

The jelly jar shook in Shade's hands. He looked down into it, face lowered, blankly studying the swirling cubes of ice until, finally, he said, "So, what do you want to do about it?"

"Aw, man," she said, then, lowering her head, she used both hands to shove him aside, the contents of his drink splashing onto his shirt as she scooted past him.

He stood there for a moment, alone, absently patting his wet shirt. Then he spoke toward the front room where she had gone, saying, "Good thing I'm wearin' black to-night, or I'd have to go change."

# 3.

When John X. Shade was twenty-three he knocked up two girls in the same summer, so he married the fourteen-year-old. Almost everyone said he'd done the right thing. They were hitched quietly before Labor Day, and the nineteen-year-old left St. Bruno, headed west, and he never had heard if she'd been carrying a son or a daughter. His bobbysoxer wife was named Monique Blanqui and soon gave birth to a son, the first of three. The boy was christened Thomas Patrick but called Tip from the start, and he'd be about forty now. After five years of staid rhythm, the next two sons were born in jump time. John X. had by then ducked out on all but the most salacious domestic responsibilities, leaving Monique to tag names on the new kids, and her tastes ran more to the Gallic than Gaelic so she'd come up with Rene, then Francois.

As John X. came rolling toward St. Bruno on the blacktop from the east, he was thinking that, so far as he knew, Monique and all the boys had stayed put here, on the west bank of the big river, leading different sorts of lives on these narrow, bumpy streets. The old bridge fed his sputtering but still moving pickup truck across the broad murky expanse of water and into town.

Etta was worn out from the five days they'd been sleeping in state parks, eating Spaghetti O's straight out of cans, trying to figure where to go. She lay against the passenger door, dirty and asleep, snoring in a sweet childish tone.

For the last hour John X. had been able to tune in the All Big Band radio station from upriver, and somehow it seemed exactly right that he was slipping back into town while Helen Forrest sang "Skylark." He'd always had a hot, hot attitude toward Helen Forrest, and listening to her now he realized that he pretty much still did.

The music of yesteryear kept playing while John X. scanned the streets, and it seemed that they were the same as in yesteryear, too. He'd lived here 'til he was fortyish, and it was on these combustible streets that he'd been a rascally kid, a nasty teen, a thief, and eventually a damned fine pool player with a major in one-pocket and a minor in nine-ball. Behind one of these storefronts he'd booked bets for Auguste Beaurain, and in a dirt alley off Lafitte Street he'd taken a straight-razor to the chest and tummy of a burly Frogtown gangster who he was forever thankful he hadn't killed. Almost every rowhouse or clump of bushes put John X. in mind of past sexual encounters. He'd rutted around this neighborhood nearly nonstop from the age of twelve and a half on up, and after Monique had put the seal of approval on him by marrying him, the opportunities came even more brazenly, mainly from her friends, in irresistible variety.

John X. drove slowly on these streets, for they were as familiar and warm to him as a mother hug. As he rolled along he spotted the vacant brick hulk that had once been The Sulthaus Brewery, a hulk his own father had trudged to and from for thirty years, six days a week, even during Prohibition, but he'd never been promoted from the loading dock. John X. slowed to look at the boarded-over entryway. Sulthaus Beer had come in black bottles with green labels, and was known for having a smoky taste. Old Thomas Parnell Shade had once saluted his only child by hoisting a black bottle and saying, "Johnny Xavier, all a man can hope for is an occasional cool drink, which I have, a clean life, which I strive for, all capped off by a Catholic burial, which I await."

John X. drove on, nodding his head, for the old man had known what he wanted, and he'd gotten it.

As the truck rolled down Fifth Street he pointed a finger toward a sign that said Hotel Sleep-Tite on a four-story brick building that used to be The Heiser House way back when, and he tingled a bit remembering Mrs. A. T. Yarborough whose husband had been mayor, and whose afternoons had been open, up there on the top floor. Christ, she must've been forty-two or three, and him half that, but, geez, he'd learned it was true, pluck those seasoned fiddles right and they'll give you back the most sonorous tunes.

There was a new traffic light on Fifth, and after he stopped at it John X. stared over at Etta, who was definitely the wild card in his life right now, and he flubbed his lips as he considered how such a wild card might best be played.

Hell, who knows?

Let *that* sink in.

When the light flashed green he drove on and Anita O'Day sang "Let Me Off Uptown," and a big sly grin came over him as he listened because there'd always been a puff or more of steam clouding his thoughts on her, too.

Man, women were a different kettle of fish in those days.

At Voltaire Street he turned right and slid into the very heart of Frogtown, the neighborhood he'd come up in, then left his first family to. He drove slowly, for he wasn't in a big toot to get anywhere in particular, and it was passing strange to be in surroundings so familiar.

A long time back John X. had fingered St. Bruno in his rearview mirror, and had only breezed through town a few times since. Seems like he saw Tip play in a high school football game where some kind of trophy was at stake, and he was positive he'd seen Rene flog the burritos out of a Texican light-heavy in an eight-rounder at the Armory. But most of his life since leaving had been spent on the road where he sought out touted young hustlers whose one-pocket nerve he wanted to test, or old reliable strokers whose nine-ball inadequacies were obvious to him but obscure to themselves. And in between such sporting encounters he basically *stole* paychecks from day job suckers who thought they turned into pool wizards by night. There had been largesse and intrigue in most every one of his evenings back then, and hustling, dice, and an occasional petticoat pension had put him up in a hotel room life, downing a bottle a day to keep things fun, dining in raffish night spots, dressing like a corn-pone Errol Flynn, tellin' all the interesting gals he met that they had somethin' special that just sang out to him, and humpin' any of 'em who grinned shyly and hopefully said, Really? There had been a sweet

string of years like that, up and down and here and gone
years, the good years before he'd turned crazy for just one
doll and ended up with Randi Tripp, the 'Bama Butterfly.

Oh, man.

Let *that* sink in.

Then, to complete his ruin, his eyes sold him downriver by going weak, and his hands joined the conspiracy
by becoming shaky.

Oh, criminentlies.

And now Lunch would be searching for him and the
kid, and that guy'd never believe the truth even if he told
it to him, which he wasn't so sure he'd do anyhow. Huh-
uh. Lunch can go piss up a rope—I've got a gun, too,
right?

That's a choice.

As John X. cruised the streets of Frogtown his eyes
alighted on reminders of his own life. He could remember
these streets under water, with channel cat and alligator
gar swimming in them. The big river had taken a notion
and bathed these streets many times, and he could chart
his life by the flood marks still visible on several of the
buildings. The black uneven band left by the '27 Flood was
the highwater mark, coming up just shy of third-story windows. Whole families had been shipped out to sea in that
one. He had a clear memory of himself standing in drizzle
on the roof of the tall Heiser House Hotel with his dad, his
dad in shock, both of them watching the rush of water,
looking for his mother. He recalled the sights and sounds,
the cows bobbing by on the swift current, belly-up and
bloated, cottages and upturned cars swirling crazily south,
and the cries of frantic livestock, dogs, and people, and the
wretched postures of dead livestock, dogs, and people
streaming past like losing bets raked in by the victorious

river. The flood was his earliest memory of life, and his only memory of his mother.

It was right about dusk, now, on a warm fall day, and he decided to cut behind Lafitte Street and drive on the cinder trail that ran beside the railroad tracks. The trail ran between huge coal bins made of withered wood and the back door of the corner joint he'd bet Monique still lived in.

They'd had some years here, in this brick rowhouse, and their boys had been raised up on this spot, mingling with the bums who flopped in the bins, learning to stay afloat by going headfirst into the big river fifty yards east of the tracks. Monique was likely in the place yet, on the ground floor, grinding out a living with three pool tables and a Dr. Pepper cooler. Though the windows were small, he thought he spied her shape in there, perched on a high stool, blowing an elaborate chain of smoke rings his way.

John X. tipped an imaginary hat toward the window, then drove on. Down the cinder lane a block or so he came to a dirt alleyway and turned up it. He gently braked next to a wooden building that had stood up to some years. There was a rusted circle of tin nailed to the alley wall, and though the advertisement could no longer be clearly read, he knew it advertised the longtime gone Sulthaus Beer. The door of the tavern had a big sign hanging over it, and on the sign there was a debauched blue catfish standing on its tailfin, smoking a cigar while leaning against a lamppost, looking like it could use a pick-me-up drink and a piece of ass.

"My, my, how do you like that?" John X. said approvingly as he looked at the sign. "The boy has kept The Catfish afloat, if it's still his."

Etta came awake and rubbed her fists to her eyes.

"Huh?" she said.

The truck motor was idling and John X. was about to move along, when a sullen and mystical fella in a black shirt, white pants, and dirty white shoes, with a fresh pink scar over his brow, passed the mouth of the alley on Lafitte, and entered The Catfish.

John X. sighed, then hunched over and turned off the engine.

"That was one of your brothers," he said.

"Say what?" Etta said, and her mouth hung open. She rubbed both hands vigorously across her femme-flattop, her face scrunched up. She then swiveled her head around and looked down the rutted alley, across the hard-bricked street, then up at the degenerate blue catfish. "Dad, where *are* we?"

"Home," John X. said. "This here is home, Etta. Let's go in and say howdy, huh?"

"You're drivin', Dad."

They climbed out of the truck and stepped into twilight on Lafitte Street. The probably dead man's clothes John X. wore had been a decent fit on Grampa Enoch, who, when healthy, had been four inches shorter and thirty pounds heavier than himself. Gray slacks highwatered upstream of his ankles, displaying white socks that drained into low-top black sneakers. His shirt was sunset orange and what was either a plummeting stork or a pirouetting buzzard was sewn over the cigarette pocket. A rumpled shroud of green plaid jacket hung off him like a public act of penance.

John X. went to the door, paused, and peered up and down the old block, squinting at a physical world that seemed to have changed only slightly. It all looked and smelled and felt the same. He cupped an unsteady hand to

one ear hoping he could still hear it, that fondly remembered din, the clang of youth against the world, and though
he heard a faint trace of that redblooded racket he felt a
certain sinking in himself, the unpleasantly sober sense of
having been possibly bluffed by life. Suckered out of one
way of living and forced to draw toward another. Perhaps
there could've been more.

Aw, que sera and so on.

It's all choices.

Let *that* sink in.

He shook a cigarette loose and shakily lit it.

"I ain't the Aga Khan, kid," he said, "but I'll sure
'nough spring for some refreshments."

He then pulled back on the door to The Catfish Bar.

# 4.

Since he never had believed that love conquers all stuff, it was a much surprised big Tip Shade who found himself walking on his knees of late, having silently said "I give" to a yellow-headed field-hippie chick who'd come down from up in the mountains. Her name was Gretel Hyslip and she was way pregnant and alone, and he'd gotten the weak knees for her when she took a seat at his bar one morning and shyly asked for a Bloody Mary with extry stalks of celery since she was a feedin' two.

Big Tip had looked at her in the light of that morning, and said, "You ain't old enough, are you?"

"There's been some who think I am," she said.

"I mean to drink," he said. He came closer for a better look. She was a kid, more or less, with a skinny face and stringy yellow hair. A scar as wide as a whipped car aerial made a diagonal welter of proud flesh across her right cheek, but it wasn't nearly as unappealing as it should have been. A colorful butterfly was tattooed on her pale shoulder skin. Her hands were red and rough from farm work, and her eyes were gray like mountain mist. The baby she was carrying bulged her out huge.

"I ain't servin' no liquor to you pregnant," Tip said. "That's regardless of your age."

"No biggie," she said, eyes down.

"You don't want your kid to be born out of you with a hangover, do you?"

"No biggie," she said again. "It's not my baby anyhow." She rubbed both hands over the bulge. "It's done been sold off."

"Uh-huh," Tip said. "I see. You stayin' over here at Mrs. Carter's house?"

Gretel nodded yup and said yup both.

So she was alone, a kid, a yellow-haired kid of field-hippie heritage with a butterfly printed on her skin, staying over here at Mrs. Carter's house, which was a sad house full of sad girls who had cut sorry deals with motherhood, and there was that scar, that strange velvety slash on her cheek, and those gray highland eyes.

Tip said, "I'll tell you what, girl—I won't serve you no liquor, but what I will do is, I will let you set right there and for free drink soda pop 'til you splash."

"Make that Dr. Pepper," she'd said back to him, "and you got yourself a friend."

Three weeks had now passed since thirsty Gretel had raised that first glass of Pepper to this friendship, and she'd been in the place about every day since, camped on the same stool, talking bashfully and bringing Tip to his knees under the tremendous weight of new feelings.

Tip Shade was a jumbo package of pock-faced bruiser, with long brown hair greased behind his ears, hanging to his shoulders. His eyes were of a common but unnamed brown hue. He tended to scowl by reflex and grunt in response. His neck was a holdover from some normal-necked person's nightmare, and when he crossed his arms it looked like two large snakes procreating a third.

He did his own bouncing.

The Catfish Bar was a place where plots were hatched. Hunkered over shotglasses and mugs, clusters of Frog-towners put their heads together and engineered simple B & E's, past-posting schemes, city hall payoffs, the stage-craft requirements of hanging paper, thefts of the new theft-proof cars, drug deals, and revenge. In this social set to have never done time was considered to be evidence of timidity, or genius.

Tending The Catfish had been Tip's all up 'til this odd romance popped in on him and romped all over his good sense. He just liked everything about Gretel, all the earthy scent he could pick up off her, her firm feel when he brushed her body squeezing by, and the many tender scenes he flat daydreamed about her, he liked those as well. She wasn't pretty in the manner of TV-pretty, and there was that pregnant aspect of her that might involve a question-able tale, but, man, she had a smile that kicked him in the belly, and the smell of a good garden.

After about a week he asked her if she'd like to do something sometime, and she said sure, and he said what is it you want to do, Gretel?

"I like things out of the blue," she told him. "Just spring it on me."

Big Tip sprung a flick on her, a corny thing about several pencil-necks and an infant, but she laughed at key moments. They went to a café for snacks and talk after, and this date was repeated more or less exactly a number of times. Over french fries and pork tenders he came to know a little bit of her story, which was mainly centered on her family life and pretty much off the beaten track. Zodiac and Delirium were words that came into the story every so often, but it took three dates before it dawned on him those were her Pa and Ma's hippie names. It seems Zodiac and Delirium had met at a Love-In or something like it that turned into a police tantrum, and out of resentment toward the laws of such society they had retreated far into the Ozark piney woods with the rest of their tribe and pitched themselves a different world right alongside the King's River. This fresh-made world was one of damned few rules and plenty of hugging and kissing and standing around naked and stoned before the eyes of various gods, but not much practical ever got done in the way of food or money or shelter, and when the third winter was whistling in, most of the tribe hustled back to the main road and thumbed toward central heating.

Zodiac and Delirium stayed behind and true to their different world, and when Gretel was born she was added to it. As Gretel grew she naturally grew weary of her parents' way of life and set out to find one that better suited her, but through a series of flukes and bad guesses that could only be called Karma, she ended up here, way downcountry, lugging a baby to market.

That was the gist of what Tip knew about Gretel, and none of it lowered her in his eyes or heart. He never referred to the baby, or the facts behind it. He didn't want to know.

What he did know was that this girl, this Gretel, had

buoyed him right up out of the narrow rut of his previous expectations.

And now, in the warm evening gloam of a fading fall day, she sat on her stool in The Catfish and read aloud from a tabloid she fancied because both the print and the stories were tall. Tip went about his business serving customers, and Gretel read in the halting, stumbling manner that was the result of her upbringing in a world that classed both schools and prisons as bummers.

She read with a speculative pause between each word.

" 'The man in the moon is as reg-u-lar as you or me,' Mrs. Willow Henry said. 'Though his heads are set close to-gether as a double'—what's this one, Tip?"

Tip was drawing a beer but, as usual, he had time for Gretel and her self-improvement exercises. He leaned across the bar and looked where her finger pointed.

"Yolk," he said. "Like eggs."

" 'Though his heads are set close to-gether as a double yolk,' " Gretel repeated, her spare hand rubbing at her belly. " 'Else-where out in space this is likely con-sidered cute but it sure e-nough spooked me at first.' " Gretel lifted her eyes from the paper and smiled. "What do you think?"

"It's amazin'," Tip said, beaming. "You are really, really, really comin' along good."

The door opened and Rene Shade came in and bellied up to the bar. It was still quiet in the joint.

"Hey, Tip."

"Hey, li'l blood. The usual?"

"Just a beer," Shade said. He sat on the stool beside Gretel. "You ain't contagious, are you, kid?"

"Nope."

"How you doin'?"

"Mellow. Purely mellow."

"I been meanin' to ask you," Shade said, "Is that butterfly there a Monarch?"

Gretel grinned and nodded.

"It's life-sized."

The door swung open again, and, framed by the twilight of the outdoor world, there stood a freakish little girl, and an old man with a strange fashion sense who looked odd but familiar. A cigarette slanted from the man's lips and he raised his shaky hands two-gun style, aimed a quivering index finger at both Shade and Tip, fanned his thumbs like triggers, then said, "Say, ain't you fellas sons of mine?"

Dark had fallen by now. The Shades were sitting at a small round table, getting sloshed as a family. The walls were adorned with athletic posters and photos, and ragged fishnets hung from the ceiling. The room was dimly lit, with shadows in the corners, and Catfish regulars were filling those shadows up. Tip's assistant, Russ, was working the bar, and Tip poured the whisky at the table near the wall.

A partly consumed triple order of frog legs sat on a platter in the center of the table. Etta and Gretel were drinking soda pop, taking turns playing the pinball machine at the back of the room.

Tip pointed at his newly discovered half sister and said, "So, we gotta add her to the Christmas list, or what?"

"Up to you," John X. said, a full glass in his hand.

Once again Tip pointed at Etta, with her flattop and purple nails and crucifix earring, and said, "John, that there is an out*landish* little kid."

John X. nodded slowly, his eyes shiny.

"All of mine have been," he said. "Far as I know."

"Uh-huh. I hear you." Tip winked at Shade, then poured more whisky into his father's glass. "So, Johnny, how the hell *are* you, anyhow?"

"My liver ain't turnin' out to be quite the organ I'd hoped for, Tippy," John X. said as he pulled the drink inside the corral his arm made upon the table. "But the thing about tears is they're salty, and salt ain't good for an ol' boy like me."

Shade sat slouched in his chair, studying his father as if trying to match him with a Wanted Poster in his mind. He'd run into him here and there over the years, but he'd never looked like this. There had always been resourceful vitality behind most of his Dad's handsome expressions, and this quality had consistently made more limp sorts want to be his friend, or at least acquaintance, to hear the colorful spectrum of his views, to lose money to him then take him home to get drunk with the wife. He'd slid through many a sporting year like that, but, man, the years had caught up and made sport of him. His hands shook, and his fingers looked like grubworms wigglin' on hooks. He was slim and all, but his skin had a bad yellow coat and his throat had deep, weathered creases in it. The old man had been tanned by the light of too many beer signs, and it just goes to show that you can't live on three decks of Chesterfields and a fifth of bourbon a day without starting to drift far too fuckin' wide in the turns.

Shade spoke up, saying, "You know, John, I've got to mention this—you really look different."

"Older you mean?"

"Not just older," Shade said, "but pretty much washed

out, too. I mean, you always used to dress so spiffy—what happened?"

"Well, now, I always used to be a beautiful, flashy sort of fella," John X. said, then brought his hands together and made a diving motion, "but lately I've taken the big *plunge* into humility."

"That's what they call it in your circle, huh?"

"Look, here," John X. said, and held his arms spread wide. "I don't expect major hugs or nothin', but a friendly drink and a likewise bit of chewin' the fat oughta be in order."

"Hallelujah to that," Tip said with a smile. He filled all three glasses with Maker's Mark, a whisky that had long comprised John X.'s main food group. He then said, "So, Johnny, what kind of hustle is it brings you back to town?"

"It's no hustle. Hell, I'm done with that. What it is, is, it's a choice."

Tip, the eldest son, stared at his pop expectantly, waiting for some sort of punchline. When none came he said, "A choice, man? Whatta you mean by choice?"

A little sip of the sour mash oiled John X.'s throat just right and he said, "In life you're always gettin' into positions where you got to make choices, boys. Read me? You go this way, you go that way, you fall down in the middle and cry like a banshee, whatever. Them's all choices, and you want to be careful with them fuckers. Be ginger with them. Try to make 'em shrewd, 'cause in later years wrong ones you made can really loom up from behind and lord it over you."

"You mean like choosin' to be a wandering drunk and gambler?" Shade asked.

John X. gave his only blue-eyed son a flat stare, then nodded.

"Exactamunto, Rene. I should've made a choice to be a priest, maybe. The hours suck, but the perks are good, eternal life and whatnot." He raised the glass of whisky, held it under his nose, closed his eyes, and inhaled the scent. "That sounds nice to me these days."

"Huh-uh," Tip said. "*Noooo*, Johnny. If you'd've chose to be a priest, we wouldn't be here, now would we?"

"No, you wouldn't. Good point. You'd've both been sticky splatters on my sheets in the mornin', at best." He turned to Shade. "Did I make the right choice after all, son?"

Before Shade could make a response two grayheaded Catfish regulars sidled up to the table and said, "Johnny Shade, is it you?" And the old man said yes to them and they were off on a series of enthusiastic comments and shoulder slaps and grins. The balder buddy was Mike Rondeau, and the other Mr. Sportin' Life of 1947 was a burly red-faced fella named Spit McBrattle who was still active enough to get an occasional mention in the police blotter. Pop Shade seemed to revel in the reunion, and he kept a Chesterfield lit at all times, firin' 'em up with that same eight-ball Zippo he'd been carrying when he dumped the family, years ago. After a few minutes John X. told Mike and Spit that he'd be around, but now he wanted to talk to his boys, and Mike said how *long*'ll you be around this time Johnny, and the answer caused Tip and Shade to lock eyes, stony faced, because it was for good, fellas, I'm home forever.

Then the sports drifted and John X. turned back to the table and said to Shade, "So, you still with the cops?"

"Vaguely."

"Vaguely? What's that mean?"

Tip grinned and cut in, "It means some of the boys in blue, plus some of the dudes with pinkie rings, are all upset with li'l blood, here."

"Oh. I'm sick of that whole stripe of people, myself," John X. said. "But I guess it can't be good for you, Rene."

"They know where to find me."

John X. then gestured at the fresh pink scar over Shade's brow. "What happened there?"

"Little trouble."

"Little trouble, huh? I hope you got paid for it."

" 'Fraid not."

"Criminentlies." John X. sadly shook his head. "I'll have to let *that* sink in. You want to get in trouble, son, you should get in trouble for profit, not just self-expression. Always remember that."

The trio of men laughed at this, and drinks were freshened all around. On the wall directly above the table, hanging from a nail, there was a framed photo of Willie Hoppe and Welker Cochran, cues in hand, exchanging sneers at the '39 Three-Cushion Billiards Championship. As the laughter faded John X. looked up at the picture and said, "Hell, Willie, Welker, I can't shoot a puppy no more."

Gretel came back from the pinball machine and stood behind Tip. She looked over her shoulder at Etta and said, "That girl plays that game tough."

"I imagine," John X. said.

"You sure do have you a nice aura," Gretel said.

"I do?" John X. said. "What's nice about it?"

She concentrated her vision on the old man.

"Why, the color. You have a purple fringe, Mr. Shade, and that's hopeful."

There was no audible response to her, and she stood heavily for a moment, then said, "I've got to head home to Mrs. Carter's now. It was good to meet you."

"I'll see her out," Tip said. "I think I'll call Francois, too. And grab us another bottle."

Tip and Gretel lumbered away, and Shade went silent, watching his father's face, a face that dragged him backward into history. On Saturday evenings in the years when John X. lived at home, and family life and liquor conspired to make him feel expansive, he would pack his three boys into the tight front seat of his already decrepit bullet-shaped '51 Ford, then slide in beside them, behind the wheel. Shoulder to shoulder, hip to hip, they rode around Frog-town. Daddy always packed six cans of beer, and the boys took turns lowering the church key that dangled from the rearview mirror, then gladly punching holes in the cans for him, the man at the wheel. Inevitably they cruised Voltaire Street where the bars and pool halls and tough guys were. Sighting a gang on the corner one day, John X. said, "Boys, I'm goin' to show you some hoodoo your daddy can work. I'm goin' to roll right past that knot of thugs over there, and I'm goin' to call ever last one of 'em an asshole, and they're goin' to smile and wave back at me." Then, with the boys big-eyed and fearful, he'd stuck his head and arm out the window, his hand holding a brew, honked the horn, and shouted, "Hey, assholes!" but slur-ring the words cheerily into a great, indecipherable, melted phrase, "Heyayasyarshehoooles!" The bug eyes of the Shade brothers fixed on the ducktailed boppers, who turned, looked at the car and their old man, and sure enough smiled at him, calling him Johnny. This became a game for the Shades alone, hurling smiley insults at hoods, red-lipped whores, hard-ass cops, thieves of all ages, and known killers, and eventually they got Greg and Slick Charbonneau, Mayor Yarborough, the Second Street Stompers, two of the Carpenter brothers, and on one occasion even Mr. B., to amiably raise a hand in acknowledgment of their salute. No insult was ever taken as John X. insulted the most dangerous folk in Frogtown, and always, as they drove on, he'd plant an elbow in the ribs of the nearest son and say, "You seen it, boys. Your daddy calls 'em assholes, and they're *happy* to hear it."

When Tip returned to the table with a fresh bottle, John X. pushed Shade's glass toward him and said, "Drink up, son."

Tip opened the new bottle and passed it around.

"I guess Frankie can't make it," he said.

John X. nodded.

"I never knew him the way I knew you two."

"Well," Tip said, "he says you've been a phantom too long to be anything else to him now. He's got some sort of grudge."

"No problem," John X. said. "He's a lawyer, right?"

"Uh-huh," Tip said. "He's doin' pretty good, too."

"Ah, well," John X. said, smiling, "I'm glad to hear that."

Etta came over from the pinball machine in the back of the room and sat on a wooden chair and scooted it up to the table. Her attire consisted of the same cut-off jeans she'd had on when they put Mobile behind them, and the same grimy green T-shirt, but the cooler air had prompted her to wear a black-and-white checked shirt of Grampa Enoch's like a sweater, and she'd ditched the thongs in favor of red sneakers. She plucked a frog leg from the platter and chomped into the meatiest part of it. Her lip color of *this* day was orange, and faint orange dabs had survived four frog legs and a soda before this, but now she smeared them off by wiping her mouth with the back of her hand. "Riv-vet. Riii-vet," she said, mocking her meal.

There was a strange, slim smile on Shade's face as he looked at this Madonna-wanna-be who had so suddenly been shuffled into the family deck.

"How'd you do on the pinball?" he asked her.

"I brung it to its knees," she said. "There's a hard tilt on that sucker, so I whupped it good." She grinned at him, and despite her attire and coif she looked ten years old. "Truthfully, it ate my quarters. I'm tapped out."

"Tapped out, huh?" Shade said, repeating the gambling term. "You're your daddy's kid, alright." He shoved a hand into his pants pocket and raised out a fistful of change which he plopped in front of her. "You're not tapped out, now, Etta. Go get even."

Etta dropped the frog leg, then used her right hand to slide the change to the table edge and held her left underneath to catch the falling coins.

"Thank you, Tip," she said.

"No, no—I'm Rene. *He's* Tip."

"Shit," she said, her head bowed. "I'm sorry."

Then she shuffled toward the pinball machine.

The bar was nearly full, smoke clouds hanging beneath the ceiling, guys in shirtsleeves and tattoos arguing about football, romance, and burglary. At the pool table in the rear a couple of young dudes in olive factory uniforms were jawing out three-foot puppy shots, then pointing at the cue ball and loudly bragging, "But look at that shape."

John X. kept glancing at them, sort of wistfully.

"Look, John," Tip said. "What're you and Etta goin' to do here? How'll you get by?"

John X. shrugged.

"I'll nibble from the big hound's bowl."

"You'll what?"

"I'll take a little from those that's got a lot."

The brothers' eyes met, then Shade said, "Okay, sport, you did it, you confused us."

"Huh. Didn't even break a sweat, neither." John X. lifted his glass and rolled it in his hands. "I'll just open a friendly poker game for me, and all the fellas like me around here. I'll offer a square gamble to old-timers, and we'll see what happens." He sighed. "I can hardly even run a single rack anymore."

"Well, hell," Tip said, his pocked face sincerely composed. "I've got room. You'n the kid can flop with me, Dad."

"That's a nice-soundin' stragedy," John X. said. "It has a nice ring to it."

Shade listened to this, and felt funny hearing it.

"You're really stayin'?"

"Oh, yeah, son. You bet."

Shade pushed his chair up close to the table. His eyes were honky-tonk red and he used both hands on his drink.

"Dad," he said, "now *why was it* you ran out on us in the first place?"

The old man's lips turned down in distaste. He glanced back to where Etta was pinging thousands of bonus points out of the pinball machine, then swung his eyes to the ceiling, then closed them.

He said, "See, fellas, long ago on a drunk night I lost my lucky penny, and ever since then I been on this endless pursuit of the one-armed man who found it and wouldn't give it back. But lately I heard on the grapevine he's turned up here again, back in the old hometown."

# 5.

Lunch Pumphrey allowed himself exactly seven cigarettes a day, and when he rolled off Rodney Chapman's wife, Dolly, he immediately reached for his pack and put fire to Salem number three. He hungrily inhaled the mentholated smoke, then collapsed onto a soft porch chair that had a fabric depicting lush orchids. He smoked for a moment, trying to get his breathing in order, his fingernails idly scraping at a lipstick smear below his belly button.

"Whew!" he said. "That sure ought've been a cure for *some*thin' or other, huh?"

"Oh, it was," Dolly said. She was still on the couch, her left hand covering her eyes, her right dangling toward the floor. Dolly was of tender years with a sour face. She had store-bought blond hair hanging in long lanks, and her body was lean from sheer youth and powdered stimulants, with an all-over golden tan and black pubes shaved down to a naughty pinch. She was ol' Rodney's young wife and she dug him plenty, but if someone fell by with some good cocaine and a dick she'd make the connection. "Boredom maybe," she said. "This could be a cure for that."

Lunch said, "I think it's a ancient one for that."

They were on the back veranda of the Chapman place, perched above the shoreline along the Redneck Riviera. Lunch got up to better appreciate the setting, for the veranda was a point with a view to offer, a vista, and he stared out across the Gulf water, squinting against the afternoon sun, his line of sight going more or less toward Panama or someplace of that type. He burned his cigarette down at a high rate, inhaling diligently, sweeping his eyes over a shimmery green expanse. There were a few motorboats and flapping sails out there. Tiny waves. Noisy birds of several sizes. Kind of interesting to look at, but not worth the real-estate prices by any stretch.

"Lunch, honey," Dolly said. "Can I get into a little more of your blow?"

"You betcha," he said. "Keep frisky."

Lunch looked like a self-portrait by an Expressionist who'd been skipping his Lithium. His face reflected a duality in that one half was clear and smooth as a babyass and the other half was bruise. His right cheek was still swollen along the jawline all the way to the ear, and in a gaudy stage of the healing process. Blue, black, yellow, purple— an awful selection of hues clashed on his face. His bodyskin was pale as fresh canvas, and numerous county-jail artists had used it as such. From his shoulders to his ankles there were perhaps six rough sketches and fifteen completed works on his skin. There was a heart with a pitchfork jabbed into it on his right bicep, a heart with a banner around it that said Yesterday on his left. Up and down his body there were skulls and lightning bolts and other sinister images that carried useful symbolic freight in the lock-ups of the world. At some point Lunch had caught on to the techniques of the Holding Tank School of Art, and with a needle and string and a bottle of ink he'd attacked the canvas of himself with no design at all in mind. One upper thigh read Repent upside down with a faint X through it, and on the other, right side up, it said Born to Raise Hell. His left forearm bore the inscription Cubs Win! His compact body was well adorned by this art, and though his interest in such artistry had resulted in an occasional infection, it had also given him many indelible memories.

The cigarette had burned down to the filter and Lunch flicked it away. He ran a hand across his sweat-dampened red hair and it stuck up in short spikes. He turned and watched Dolly hunker over the coke tray, her nose down, snorting up a drug-hog portion.

"Mmm," she went, her eyes shining.

"Uh-*huh*," Lunch said. He shook his head in wonder at her simplicity. She seemed to think he was merely colorful or raffish or strangely cute or some such, and, really, she should look deeper'n that. She should look deeper'n that and recognize a few terrible qualities in him, and right away, too.

She was still beaming when the front door slammed.

Her eyes started to spin in her head and she nervously looked to Lunch, who said calmly, "I expect that'll be your husband."

She let go with a long, high-pitched whimper of panic, and before the sound of it faded Rodney Chapman showed up in the doorway, an empty wine bottle held in his hand like a club, his hand shaking. He stared at her for a long second, then moaned and spun away, this spin bringing naked Lunch into view.

Their eyes met and Lunch said, "You should've just took my calls, man—you know I'm remorseless this way."

Rodney's eyes began to water. His mouth hung open. He said, "Lunch."

On the floor of the veranda was the black wad of Lunch's undies. He put his left foot over the wad, clenched his toes, and, with a display of simian dexterity, raised the undies to his hand. After he stepped into the bikini briefs, he said, "Where is he?"

"He? Who, he?" Rodney said. Rodney Chapman had rounded the age of forty a few years back, and he had a rounded shape, sparse brown hair, and a simple story. Until that fortieth year he had tended his mother as she died, an act that, owing to her moral vigor and pioneer genes, had taken nearly two decades to be finalized. Her strength just went down by the thimbleful from year to year, and Rodney had no special life outside the abject duty of tending her until mommy *did* bite it, leaving him behind in this world with only considerable personal wealth to compensate for the loneliness. Being a man alone in the world with considerable personal wealth seemed to change the way all the eyes on the planet focused, for suddenly he was no longer seen as merely a kind of patrician nerd, but a fascinating throwback to a more genteel era. Many a glossy gal heard his tale from himself or others and jumped on him with smiles ablaze and skirts lifted, relentlessly employing their charms. Dolly was one of the bronzed babes who saw him as the fabled main chance, and after a year he married her because she was the most inventively aggressive. In her arms he became a different man. Life brightened up and he acquired sensual vices. He grew a fluffy mustache and kept his fingernails trimmed down smooth. Now, on this sad afternoon, he looked at Dolly there on the couch, where she lay naked, crying gently, still wet from another man's kisses, and he felt the entire fantasy of his new self just fall to pieces and scatter on the veranda.

"Where is he?" Lunch asked again. "Where the hell is ol' Paw-Paw?"

Rodney deflated visibly, his shoulders sagging, chest heaving, head dropping. He wore a light blue sports coat over a deep blue shirt, with black slacks and shoes. He slumped to a soft chair, eyes down, and let the wine bottle fall from his hand.

He said, "Did John do that to your face?"

Lunch put his snap-brim black hat back on and said, "I ain't after pity, man—it's answers I'm here for."

Ever since Mother Chapman passed on Rodney had made attempts to be outgoing and upbeat and a man about town, more or less, but after a few months he'd narrowed the town he was about down to just Enoch's Ribs and Lounge. He sat at the bar there most nights, sipping Chablis, listening to the 'Bama Butterfly, gabbing with roguish John X., the widely traveled night bartender, for from three to six hours a visit.

"I didn't even know John was leaving," he said.

"He did it of a sudden I think," Lunch said.

Dolly sat up on the couch, found her yellow sundress on the floor, and pulled it on. She sniffled loudly several times, then stamped her bare feet on the floor, banging out a fleshy tom-tom solo.

"Why are you here?" she asked Rodney when her heels began to hurt.

"Pardon?"

"At *this* time. Why are you here at *this* time?"

Rodney looked at his wife, his face giving expression to queasy thoughts his mouth just couldn't quite get around to uttering. Finally, he said, "The neighbors."

"The *neigh*—bors?"

He nodded.

"The neighbors called me at the club because their children, their little-bitty children, could see you out here, you know, cavorting."

Dolly raked her hands through her long blond hair and growled.

"The neighbors! The neighbors! I'll burn their fuckin' house down, little-bitty children and all!"

Lunch was calmly standing there on the sunny veranda in his bikini briefs and snap-brim hat, apparently amused.

"Looky here, Dolly," he said, "don't go blaming your neighbors for that phone call, 'cause, actually, it was me." He pointed at Rodney. "You never returned any of the calls I made to you, man. You knew I'd be after ol' Paw-Paw, your pal, so your answering machine quit knowin' me."

Dolly helped herself to a Salem from Lunch's pack and lit up. She exhaled severely.

"When did you call him? I don't remember you goin' anywhere near the goddamn phone."

"You were in the shower, darlin'," Lunch said. "So you'd taste fresh—remember?"

The man of the house began to sob upon hearing this culinary detail, his rounded shoulders bouncing with each breath.

Dolly watched her hubby weep, then said, "You bastard. You son of a bitch. I used to think you were a nice little dude with a big unfair reputation hung on him, but now I know better."

"You still don't know the half of it," Lunch said. "But you might before I leave here."

Still sobbing, Rodney picked up the wine bottle. He chopped the air with it a few times, saying, "Why, I. Why, I oughta. Splat! Yes, sir. Why, I."

"Hey," Lunch said, "y'all can get into your conjugal boo-hoos later." He pointed at his clothes sticking out from the chair seat beneath Rodney. "I don't want to tempt you by comin' over there, son—so just hand me my britches, huh?"

Rodney, still seated, raised the wine bottle like he might throw it at Lunch.

"Oh, no, don't," Dolly said. "Don't!" She scooted across the sun-dappled veranda and touched her husband lightly on his chest. "Don't do it, baby—Lunch'll kill you. He's known for that."

"That's good advice she's giving you," Lunch said. "I oft times *do* have a place in the life cycle, when money's at stake. So cool your jets down and drop that bottle." The bottle dropped. "Now be the gentleman you are, Rodney, and kindly hand me my Levi's. And pick 'em up by the belt loops, so you don't dump my pocket change all over the floor, here."

Dolly's fingertips were still touched to Rodney's chest. He looked up at her, then looked down and swatted her fingers away. She went back to the couch and he stood. He grabbed the belt loops and handed Lunch his Levi's. Then he handed him his shirt.

"Here's your shirt," he said.

Lunch started dressing.

Dolly was curled up in a yellow ball on the couch, her

legs tucked beneath her, her head bowed. She said, "It's time to face up to it—I have a problem. A *serious* problem."

"So where is he?" Lunch asked.

Storm clouds had mobbed up out over the Gulf and were quickly rumbling toward shore.

Once again seated and moist in the eyes, Rodney said, "I don't really know. He's from over there in bayou country. The town is called, I think, St. Bruno. Upriver from N'Awlins. Some distance. When he said home, that's where he meant."

"I've heard of that place," Lunch said. "Reckon that's where he'd go?"

"It's a *serious* problem," Dolly said, "and the very first step is admitting that I have it."

"Who knows?" Rodney said. "It's all I can tell you." He looked at Dolly but spoke to Lunch. "I guess you just had to do this. You just had to ruin my life."

"Looky here now," Lunch said. Lunch had his pants on and his black shirt hung down unbuttoned. He was bent over, zipping up his half-boots, his black hat bobbing. "It's like the dyin' old men all over the world will tell you, Rodney—when you get aged and rackety and think back across your entire life span, why, it ain't the ones you do you regret, it's the ones you don't."

"Is that so?" Rodney said.

"It sure is." Lunch brushed lint from his pants leg as he stood up. "I mean, a piece of tail is a piece of tail, and your wife is purty cute, and she'd be one I'd sure 'nough regret someday if I didn't. You *could* take that as a compliment, you know."

"*Honey?*" Dolly said. "*Baby?* You know I love you, don't you? You know I love you, but I don't know if *you* love *me*, love me enough to help me fight this awful thing, my addiction."

Rodney turned to stare at her.

"That's what my problem is," she said. "My *serious* problem. I'm an addict—I couldn't face up to it before. But a thing like this, here, today, why, it's only my addiction that could bring me this low, bringing me to betray the love we have, honey, all 'cause of my sick, sick, sick addiction to nose candy."

Lunch got his cigarettes and coke from the table, pausing to grin a huge one down at Dolly.

Rodney kept staring at her.

"Drug troubles are tough to lick, but with you by my side I *could* fight this thing. Drugs *can* be beat, baby. Will you stand by me while I fight this thing?"

Rodney said, "You've just lain with Lunch, here, in *my* house, and you want to know if I'll stand by you?"

"It's a *disease*," she said plaintively. "What has happened here proves how *sick* I am from it. Sick, sick, sick." She brought her hands up to her face and began unleashing tears behind them. "I'm *addicted*—I *need* you, I *need* you, I *need* you, to help me fight it."

Rodney wiped a stubby finger at a tear on his cheek.

"We'd cut out all the *co*-caine?" he asked.

"Uh-huh."

"No more toot and brandy breakfasts?"

"Huh-uh."

"We'll stay away socially from bad influences?"

"Mmm-hmm."

Dolly was still sending forth tears from behind her hands.

"We'd have to do all those things," he said, "to have

a chance. Any chance at all. And might as well kick beer, too. It's just a stepping stone. And French wines and pot—they'll have to go."

Dolly let her hands fall away from her damp sour face.

"French wines and pot aren't hurting anything much, honey," she said in an instructive tone. "The surest way is to *ease* out from under an addiction, not go cold turkey."

Real sharp laughter came from Lunch.

"Hoo, hoo, hoo!" he went. "Rodney, ol' son, I don't believe you can handle a gal like this one here. Hoo, hoo! She's from places like where *I* come from. She's fixin' to make herself seem codefendant with good blow, man—like she wouldn't've shook hands with me otherwise." Lunch adjusted the snap-brim hat on his head. "She's from the level I know well, which is one where you've got to be hard on her, or she'll just cook your ass down to mush, ol' buddy. You've got to whomp a gal like her to get any respect. Make her lips swell up tight for a spell." Rodney kept looking down, so Lunch cupped a hand beneath his pudgy chin and raised his face until their eyes met. "You've got to be a man, son—you can't let her bullshit you like this." He pinched Rodney's cheek to a red glow. "Be a *man*."

The storm clouds above the Gulf cut loose, and over on the couch Dolly clamped her jaws and looked fierce.

The condom Lunch had used was on the floor beside the couch and she picked it up, then twirled it like a slingshot.

"Hey, Lunch," she said, "Eat scum and die."

Lunch sensed something en route toward his head and turned enough that the projectile merely skimmed his hat brim, then swirled down to land on Rodney's shoe.

THE ONES YOU DO

The contents oozed across the imported leather on his toes.

Rodney began to weep instantly. Ingrained manners caused him to promptly ease a white hankie from his breast pocket and clumsily wipe at his shoe.

Lunch stared down at Rodney, whose sobbing reaction displayed how little manly advice he'd absorbed, then shook his head in disgust, and threw his hands up in a gesture of defeat. He started stomping toward the door, saying, "Son, you are fuckin' *hope*-less!"


The parking lot at Enoch's Ribs and Lounge was empty except for a few beer cans and paper litter. A sign in the window of the dark restaurant said Closed For Remodeling.

Lunch parked his VW Bug in the shade of a large oak tree so the late afternoon sun wouldn't cook his bucket seats, then let himself into Enoch's through the front door. The front room was shadowy, with a musty odor in the air. Chairs were upturned and stacked on tables, and vast cobweb empires were expanding in the upper reaches of the room.

About halfway across the room Lunch heard the sound of cooking, and then the smell became distinct also. The grill was on in the kitchen. Lunch bent down to his left boot and came up with a two-shot derringer. He quietly crossed the lounge to the kitchen and slowly pushed the swinging doors aside, and there at the grill stood Short Paul of Tampa, spatula in hand, tending to a brace of T-bone steaks.

Short Paul looked at Lunch and said, "No potatoes?

I searched all over and couldn't find none nowhere. Not even frozen."

"Huh," went Lunch.

"I'm a person who keeps it simple, you know—with meat, why, you have potatoes. Maybe peas or a salad or somethin', too, but those're extras." Short Paul was of a regular size but many times in his youth he'd come up short on his bar tab, hence the nickname. He had abundant gray hair brushed straight back from a jolly face that got him fast, friendly service from café waitresses with marital woes. A big-city growl snapped at the heels of his words, and he had the skin-tone of a beachfront condo owner. "But potatoes ain't an extra with meat—they're a must."

Lunch put the derringer in his front pocket, then calmly lit Salem number four.

"You here to lean on me?"

"I would never try to *lean* on *you*."

"You should make that never, never, never."

"Hey, now, be cool," Short Paul said with a quick grin. "Angelo and me, we just want our money."

Lunch looked at the T-bones cooking on the grill, then stared quizzically at Short Paul.

"No p'taters, huh?"

"None nowhere."

"That meat come out of my freezer?"

"Mm-hmm. You don't mind, do you?"

Lunch shook his head, smoke curling from his nostrils.

"Course not—help yourself."

After flipping the meat, Short Paul said, "That dude sure jacked your face up, Lunch. When will it be back to normal?"

"He japped me with a bottle, Short. Doctor said I was lucky nothin' broke."

"I guess," Short Paul said. "But, let me tell you, it don't look good, what he done."

Lunch eased over next to Short Paul, then flicked cigarette ashes on Short's yellow shirt.

"I need a ashtray," he said. "You'll do."

"Hey, hey," Short Paul said, backing away, swatting at the ashes. "Don't forget who I'm *with*, Lunch! Don't forget the people I'm with, pal."

Lunch wagged his head and smiled. "I'm only with my lonesome," he said. "But I still consider *me* to be the majority in most *any* argument."

"Yeah. That's what you're famous for." Short Paul downshifted in mood, allowing his composure to catch back up to him. The T-bones were sizzling so he raised the spatula and dished the meat onto a white plate. "So, Lunch," he said, "you still number your smokes?"

"Yup." Lunch was savoring the last puff of number four, leaning against the wall, letting the smoke float from his mouth only to be reinhaled through his nostrils. "Us smaller fellas has to keep our bad habits on short leashes. We can't run wild with 'em and still stack up in a pinch the way your moose-type of fella can." Lunch spit on the end of the cigarette, then dropped the butt. "Plus, seriously, there's nature, which I don't feel we should smoke all up just out of habit. Really, seven cigarettes a day is all you want, except out of habit."

Short Paul nodded, then pointed with the plate, gesturing toward the lounge.

"Let's grab a seat," he said, "while I have a bite. I gotta drive back to Tampa yet."

"Where's your Caddy?" Lunch asked as they sat at a table.

"In the alley."

"How'd you get in here?"

"Well, you have a window to fix, back there, by the alley."

Short Paul carved the meat from both T-bones into little mouthfuls, then started spearing them and eating them like he was being timed for speed.

"I found where the man might've gone," Lunch said. "His hometown was this place, you know, over in the bog country there, swamps and all that. I heard of it before, they call it St. Bruno."

Nodding and chewing in concert, Short Paul spat out, "Sure. Gamblin' town. Used to play cards up there."

"You what?" Lunch asked.

Short Paul, within sight of victory over his steaks, dropped his fork, then breathed deeply.

"I used to go there for the Hold 'Em games, years ago, when the snow pigeons had flown back to Ohio and stuff. I got to know this guy, dangerous sort of a wise guy over there, name of Ledoux. Pete Ledoux." Short Paul put both hands over his belly, then made a sour face. "If he wasn't dead I could call him, ask him if he knows this old man—Shade, ain't it?"

"John X. Shade."

"Pete was well connected up there." Sweat began to pour down Short Paul's forehead. His facial skin began to tune in to a less healthy color. "But a cop whacked him. Oh, man." He lifted the plate and sniffed what was left of the meat. His face bore a concerned and slightly green expression. "This smell right?"

Lunch leaned across the table and sniffed.

"Not exactly," he said. "A tad ripe, I'd say."

"It was in *your* freezer. Frozen solid."

"Yeah, well." Lunch shrugged. "The freezer was out for near a week. I just turned it on again last night."

"A week!" Short Paul raised the plate up high and hurled it across the room. He mopped his brow with a napkin. His pale green cheeks trembled. "You let me eat *rotten meat?*"

A smile played across Lunch's face. He turned his small shoulders inward in an almost coy manner.

"I couldn't be *sure* it was rotten," he said. "Course *now* I *am* sure, or purty close to it, from the look on you."

"You let me eat it!"

"I said, help yourself, that's all. And I meant it, like— eat at your own risk."

A very leery quality had taken over from Short Paul's normal jolly expression. He watched Lunch from the corners of his eyes.

"The meat was my mistake," he said softly. "Just get us our money. That's all we want."

"You'll get it, plus ol' Paw-Paw's head on a stick."

"Uhhh, forget the head on a stick. Angelo can get heads on sticks all day long, at wholesale." Short Paul choked something back down in his throat. "What he wants is his money, forty-seven K. When'll you be off to get it?"

Lunch touched a finger to his nose as if imagining his journey, then sprang from his seat, put both hands next to Short Paul's ears, snapped his fingers, and said, *"Poof!"*

With the sun sinking orange and fantastic directly in his path, Lunch cruised down two-lane blacktop, headed toward the big river that split the nation. He stayed well within the double-nickel speed limit, partly because it was a point of pride to never seem in a hurry, for any reason at any time, but also because he didn't like to put strain on his VW Bug. The Bug was red with a black interior, and he'd been driving it since his seventeenth year back in the Appalachian hills, when he'd been given it by a neighbor who didn't want any more of his hogs disappearing and figured that if the Pumphrey kid had some wheels he just might take to snatching shoats a little farther down the road.

The Bug had previously been in a smash-up, a one-car deal where a tourist from the low country refused to believe that the mountain lane he was on could possibly curve any more times in succession than it already had, and thereby missed one, shooting the Bug into a tree. Over a period of months Lunch lavished himself on the car, and tinkered it back into smooth-running shape. He polished it up 'til it glowed, and if his family had ever had anything that could by some stretch be called a *jewel*, then the Bug was it. The car fit him in every way; it was just his size, it cornered like a snake on those hillbilly highways, the colors of it spoke to him, and, naturewise it was gentle on the world, with good mileage per gallon and clean exhaust.

Nature was a force Lunch felt compelled by, both as an observer and a participant. His fondest memories were of watching puppies and calves being born on the farm back home, and of the ferocious and sweet vibrations that hummed through his arms and legs, his brain and vital organs the first time he'd killed a man. It had been for money, so that humming in his veins hadn't been venom or spleen, but an inner, almost musical sense of being connected to the natural order, linked very high up on the chain of things.

Like an owl, sort of, when it hoots in the dark.

When Lunch contemplated the life he'd been raised up in back among the Appalachians, it seemed like some dreamily remembered folk-ballad, a folk-ballad that was lunatic in spirit, for the way he recalled the years back there was that they were full of ominous moonscapes where phantasm hounds and poltergeist ancestors gave out unearthly cries from the nearby hollers, and voices of the congregated dead chewed the fat in his ear every night at bedtime, while his actual daylight life was oppressed by his grandma and aunt, who lamented his vile birth and administered constant Bible thumpings to his head to shoo away the evil he'd inherited.

Only his older sister, Rayanne, turned out at all well in his memories. It was Rayanne who would slowly check his head for lice, or lance painful boils on his childish ass, or bundle him and light candles for him when the electricity was shut off, or remember his birthday.

Even though Rayanne had often mocked or taunted him, she'd still come closest of anyone to being good to him, and when he was old enough he went to work pimping for her in Charleston, and eventually she arranged the first hit contract for him, sending him after a tavern owner in Marietta who thought he needn't listen to reason from a whore.

Man, Lunch thought, that hummin', that sweet music in the veins, it comes back over you at totally unpredictable times.

He lit Salem number five, and traced the present humming back a week or so, he thought, to the hospital and his visit to Enoch Tripp. He'd had questions for Enoch, but Enoch had had better questions for him. The old dude looked like hell, and the nurse said they'd given him something to take his mind away from all this. His eyes were wide but he hadn't seemed to recognize Lunch, his silent partner, at all.

Where are they? Lunch had asked, and Enoch had thrashed around a little and said, Second Grade. All in Second Grade now that Uncle Sam found his kittens. Do you get one?

There were tubes of oxygen going into Enoch's nose. His skin hung off him loose like a borrowed suit.

Where did ol' Paw-Paw Shade light out for? Lunch asked in a crooning voice. Where are they?

Would you sit by me? Enoch had said. Won't you set here by me and spell somethin' out plain the way you do?

Lunch had reached over and slid the tubes from the old coot's nose. Then he pinched the nostrils together, and Enoch's eyes got big, and bigger, then, of a sudden, they went peaceful, and he nodded.

Lunch let go, and the old man gasped until he reinserted the tubes. Enoch's eyes calmly followed him the whole time.

Maybe forty Japs I did in, Enoch said. Is that too much on account?

Forty? Shit, man, that's a lot. I was too young for 'Nam, and forty, man, that's a bunch in peacetime.

The old man's eyes studied Lunch from a far place.

Looky here, Lunch said, I *could* do you, 'cause I think you know I'm here, and why and all, but doin' you now would be for nothin'. Lunch leaned over Enoch, tugged his beard, and whispered, 'Cause, Enoch, nature is already killing you in a worse way than I could ever dream up.

No, sir, I couldn't improve on it, not in a hundred years of tryin'.

Salem number five was down to the filter, and Lunch stuck it in the ashtray, then kept on cruisin' west in the Bug with that music still hummin' in his veins, unblinking eyes watching the golden sun smother beneath the black horizon.

# part ii

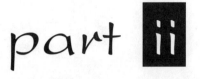

Sinking in

# 6.

"It seems I've been backin' this same king-high nada all night long," John X. Shade said as Spit McBrattle pulled in another pot. "Time to change the game."

The deal had worked its way around the table once more, back into the control of John X. He named Draw as the game because, he said, he suddenly liked the very notion of having more than one chance to catch a winning hand. All of the old and unnecessary fellas sitting around the table nodded, winked, or sighed at his comment, for at their time of life the sweet dream of more than one chance was often indulged, though scenes in it sometimes deviated uncontrollably from the benign and lush toward the numbing and stark.

The cards were shuffled and dealt in the front room of Tip's bachelor heaven, a place of rough wood and stained rugs, set atop stilts near the river, with an oil-drum dock floating on the water. The summer was long gone but a straggling day of heat had strayed into early autumn and warmed the sunlit hours, and even at this hour of the night a nice summery breeze was breathed in through the screened windows.

"Criminentlies," John X. said as he folded his hand. "So much for extra chances." He leaned away from the table and stretched his arms. "Anybody for a beer?"

Spit, red faced and riding a good streak, raised his brown bottle and held it toward his host.

"I'm ready," he said. "Suds are goin' down cool this evenin'."

John X. took the bottle and held it out to his side. He looked over by the screen door to where Etta knelt on a rug playing Solitaire, her hair ruffling in the draft, her green lips pursed in concentration as she cheated the pee-waddy-doo out of ol' Sol, the lonely cardsharp's constant nemesis. Sol hadn't a chance the way the kid flexed the rules on him, and when she smirked in victory her lips looked like a twisted dollar.

"Angel," he said to her, and as she looked up he wagged the bottle. "One for Spit."

Etta hopped up and took the empty into the kitchen.

The kitchen of Tip's bachelor heaven was solidly square in shape, with the static atmosphere of a museum exhibit. Things gleamed from cleanliness and lack of use. The shelves were severely ordered, with canned goods in tight ranks, arranged in ascending value from pure vegetables, to vegetable soups, to basically vegetable soups with *some* meat, to meat soups with *some* vegetables, on up to the head of the parade, Spam. Next to the vintage stove a neat stack of white paper plates sat on the sideboard, but above the sideboard there were red-labeled cans brimming with congealed grease drippings, lined on the window sill like potted flowers that blossomed forth a porcine fragrance. The refrigerator was shiny white, huge, and of some historical interest but also defunct, so the beer was in a gray washtub on the floor, classically chilled by large blocks of ice.

Etta dropped a hand into the ice tub and fished out a beer. She wiped the bottle dry on a towel and twisted the cap off. When she set the bottle beside Spit, she used a new monetary term she'd learned, saying, "That'll be eight bits."

Spit held the dollar bill up and she snatched it from his fingers, then went back to her cards.

"That's three bucks to you, Johnny," Mike Rondeau said. "So shit or get off the pot."

"Guess I'll shit," John X. said, and tossed in three ones.

The players kicked two bucks an hour apiece to John X. for hosting, plus he had the concession business. Etta had made sandwiches modeled on the ones Dagwood ate in the funny papers and sold them for two bucks apiece, and that had added up, along with the beer sales. So far John X. was down about twenty from poker, but up fifteen or so overall.

On this particular hand John X. had stayed to the end with two pair, treys and eights, but lost to the three fives Spit held in ambush.

"Oh, man," John X. said with a groan. "I keep gettin' tripped up by the sin of pride."

"That's not the sin that used to trip you," fat Mike said, his bald head bobbing.

"No," John X. said as he lit a Chesterfield. "That one

used to be hid so far down the list I didn't snap to it even bein' on there."

So this was the foreseeable future, hosting a weekly poker game for a pack of cranky old hounds who'd never quite caught up to the golden rabbit, but couldn't stop yapping about how close, how tantalizingly close they'd come. They'd all grown up in Frogtown during years long gone by, and most had done this and that when wars or trade carried them to various distant parts of the map to experience the life of other spots, but soon or late, for any or all of the possible reasons, they'd come back to this, the neighborhood of their youth, to live out the string.

The All Big Band radio station played constantly behind the conversational hubbub, and every second or third song one or another of the swing era swains would close his eyes and float off from this actual night, called away by the siren sounds of Kay Kyser or Les Brown or Claude Thornhill, catching slow boats to China in their minds, on sentimental journeys, having Sunday kinds of love.

And when the aged eyes of John X., Spit, Mike, or Mike's widowed brother-in-law, Stew Lassein, or Stew's widowed neighbor, Horace Nash, would slowly open once again to this place and time, they'd give their heads a shake and say something like, "Oh, *brother*, we had *music* back then."

The night air was warm as an illicit cuddle, and Spit was dealing Hold 'Em, his thick fingers flying like Benny Goodman's on a clarinet while that very instrument and man made music over the radio, and John X., feeling the warmth *and* the music, said, "What the hell, angel—free beer all around."

Etta fetched the beers to the table, then, as the old fellas raised the bottles, she said, "Ice cold beer on a sweaty day sure 'nough proves there once was saints afoot on this earth."

Mike, fat, bald, and pale, looked closely at Etta, then said to John X., "Where's a kid get stuff like *that*?"

John X. winked at his daughter.

"Me," he said. "She's a little echo of my own words."

Etta put her arms around her old man's neck, her green lips near his ear, and said, "I got you memorized."

"That's a scary thought," he said. "I think I won't have it." He reached up and jerked a rat tail of her hair, pulling her head back. "Now go away, we're gamblin'."

*"Huh,"* she grunted, then went over to the couch and stretched out, watching him.


A little after ten the All Big Band radio station called up "Pennsylvania 6-5000" and changed the tempo of the night. The recently widowed Stew Lassein was on the receiving end of that musical number, and as it played he turned to fat Mike, his dead wife's brother, and said, "You remember? That was Della and me's song."

This song and comment came up in the middle of a stud hand dealt by Spit.

"I remember," Mike said, looking down.

Stew, a naturally fair man faded by age to the very edge of transparency, went misty in the eyes.

" 'Pennsylvania 6-5000,' she'd say to me, anytime we talked, on the phone, or at night, or, really, any ol' time, and it meant, 'I got your number, and you, you got mine.' " Stew turned his wet eyes on John X. and said, "But I guess you knew that, Johnny. I would guess you knew her favorite songs."

"Can't say that I did," John X. said. Certainly can't say that it was that one, specifically. Della did like music, and she liked to do everything to musical strains, from drinking coffee along with "String of Pearls," to chewin' the sheets in tune to "Sugar Blues." There always had to be a song playin' backup to the actions in the life of pretty li'l Della Rondeau, even after she became Della Lassein. "That was a popular song, though—every juke had it."

Stew wiped a finger at his wet eyes, then his lips drew back into a snarl.

"I s'pose I look like I believe that," he said. "I s'pose I look like the sort who'll believe anything."

"Are we playin' cards, or what?" Spit said.

"Aw, please, Stew," Mike said as Stew's eyes began to leak, "would you please quit it? Just stop it." He shrugged apologetically toward the other players. He turned his hands up. "Della only died this last winter. He's still kind of raw."

"Let's play around him," Spit said. "Your jack is high, Nash."

Horace Nash, Stew's neighbor, also widowed and lean and cranky, looked at the tears and said, "Fold."

At the part of the song where the band chants "Pennsylvania six, five, oh-oh-oh," Stew Lassein responded by trumpeting a muted sob solo.

Fat Mike grimaced. He hung his head, then said, "Johnny, you remember my kid sister, Della, don't you?"

John X. studied the tears running down Stew's face. He couldn't look away from them. They irrigated the dry old skin of Lassein's cheeks, the weeping and sobbing strangely taking years off the old man for a few seconds at a time. As the tears glistened on his reddening cheeks and his body lunged along with the sobs, the old man looked alive, and lucky in his ability to grieve.

"Sure I do," John X. said. "Her and Monique were close back then." His gaze did not shift from Stew's face as he spoke. "I remember Della as this short, dark, imported-lookin' sort of dame, who had a stylish way of smokin' a Sweet Caporal, and wore feathery hats cocked on her head like a double-dare. Mm-hmm, I remember."

"That's enough!" Stew said. His lips trembled and he pointed a finger at his host. "Enough! Don't say another thing you remember about my wife!"

Spit slammed his hand on the table.

"Look," he said, "I got eleven bucks in this pot, and if y'all don't quit your crab-assin' and *play*, I'm gonna call myself winner and rake it in. I mean it—I'm here to gamble."

Stew scooted his chair back from the table. He wiped at his eyes with a party napkin, then blew his nose on it.

"I remember she liked to go to dances," John X. said, "and she always showed up at 'em with Stew, here."

The radio had moved on to a new tune, some sort of discombobulatin' rhythm from abroad, probably Cuba. The brass section was agitated and the drummers pounded out a tropical war beat.

"There," Horace Nash said consolingly to Stew, "a new song."

"I told him," Stew said, repeating the finger pointing as he spoke, "not to say *another* word about her."

"Please," Mike said, shaking his head.

"I win," Spit said. "Time's up."

He started to pull in the pot, but John X. grabbed his hand.

"Huh-uh," John X. said. "I got seven bucks in there, too." John X. folded his hands on the table and sat up straight. "Alright now, Stew—what's your beef with me?"

"Look at him," Stew said. He tossed the damp napkin onto the table. "Would you look at him? Mister Blue-eyed Innocent." Stew stood up and angrily waved a hand at John X. "I can't be around you. I thought I could. I sure thought I could, but I just can't."

"What *is* your problem with me?"

"You know what! Mister Snake-hips! You always dressed like you were *so*, so special, peddlin' lies to every girl in town, actin' so handsome! Spendin' money like you didn't have to work for it—which you didn't!"

John X. lit a Chesterfield and eased back in his chair. His hands hung loose to his sides and he said, "I never felt like I had to apologize for bein' a *dream*boat."

This statement was at the heart of the matter, it rung true, and Stew fell back on weeping. His shoulders shook and he tried to stammer a retort but gave up after, "I, I, I . . ."

Horace Nash stood up next to Stew.

"I wish I missed my Luann like you miss your Della," he said. "Yes, sir, I wish I could work up some tears for that crocodile—if I could it'd mean my life once had *some* goddamned thing of value in it." As Stew jerked and moaned he patted him on the shoulder. "I envy you, buddy. I really do."

"Criminentlies."

"You and me'll split this," Spit said, then began counting the pot.

Etta had been dozing on the couch, but now she came awake and sat up.

"What?" she mumbled. "Who?"

"I just can't take you," Stew said. "I think you know why."

The old man was then led out the door by Horace Nash.

John X. watched the screen door smack shut, then said to Mike, "Hope he gets home safe."

Mike had a fresh cigar in his mouth, unlit, and he rolled it from cheek-to-cheek, talking around it.

"I never married," he said, "so I'll drive 'em on home." Fat Mike walked to the door and said "Sorry" as he went out.

Etta got up from the couch and stood before the screen door, taking in the night breeze. Bird noises sounded from high in the tall dark trees along the river. The breeze was scented with fermenting river stink.

"Dad," she said, "what's goin' on?"

Burly Spit tossed a wad of bills John X.'s way.

"There's your split," he said. He raised his bottle of beer for a long drink. "We'll get some players who ain't so temperamental next time."

"How's *your* wife?" John X. asked.

"Oh, she's dead, Johnny." Spit rose from his chair, stretched his back, and yawned. "Seven or eight years back. Pamela couldn't resist a bargain, you know, so she overdid the stingers durin' Happy Hour at The Oasis one night. It was foggy. She run the Buick right into the bridge pilings on River Road."

"Criminentlies," John X. said. "Sorry to hear that."

"Aw, hell, I rubbed a brick on it years ago," Spit said. He slowly stepped to the door, pausing at the screen to inhale deeply. "Ol' Stew should find hisself a good brick and give it a try." He shoved the door open and stepped onto the porch. "Catch you later, Johnny."

When the door smacked shut this time, John X. leapt from his chair and lunged for the couch and collapsed. With quivering hands he lit a smoke, inhaled needily, and coughed, his entire body arching as he hacked.

Etta sat on the couch beside him. Her little hand touched his knee.

Oh, but things were sinking in. Women you'd loved when they were young, had grown old and wide and infirm, and already died of natural causes. Women younger than yourself, and beautiful.

Criminentlies, but doesn't that make the ticking clock an ominous fuckin' bully to your mind?

"Dad, why ever did that man cry so?"

Thirty-five years back, him and Della, it was a summer thing, a summer fling, maybe part of the fall, and that one time the following year. He'd had a hideaway above Verdin's Grocery, a tiny room with a Murphy bed and a radio and a back entrance from the alley, up one flight of stairs. Della was sort of beautiful, prettier when she spoke 'cause she said the damnedest things, and somehow they got together and began to meet above Verdin's, usually in the afternoon while Stew loaded trucks at Bruns Van Lines. It was always hot, no fan, but plenty of music and slick sweaty skin. The day Della first tried to call it off the temp was a delta ninety-five, and they'd watered the sheets before laying on top of them. I shouldn't be here, she said. Monique is my friend, ever since grade school. Della was dark skinned and plentiful, full of sass and never pissy, and she lay on the wet sheets belly-down, her skin moist and available. I shouldn't be here. I don't know why I do this. And John X. had sucked an ice cube from his gin and tonic into his mouth, then leaned over her, his tongue pushing the ice cube down her spine, over the hump to the crack of her ass, and he'd held the ice cube there with his tongue and slipped a finger between her thighs, lightly fingering the slit. She growled, Oh, Johnny, and he swallowed the ice cube and said, You're rememberin' *why* now, ain't you?

Etta began to shake him.

"Dad? Dad?"

"What, kid?"

"Why ever did he cry?"

After two dismal, stalling puffs John X. patted her young, bony back, and said, "Kid, I'll tell you, when someone you give two hoots about goes away for good, why, it's a thing that can shake you hard and leave cracks behind in you."

While contemplating this, Rosetta Tripp Shade folded her bare arms across her chest, her big 'Bama browns staring out a screened window toward Europe, then said, "How far off is France in hours?"

# 7.

The Lassein home was small and square, painted white, bought on a lifetime plan, and not quite paid for. When Stew got out of his brother-in-law's car he didn't say good-night, but walked briskly up the dark stone walkway and into his house. He began to turn on lamps, first one, then two, then all of them; six in the front room, three in the big bedroom, two in each of the kids' rooms, then the tall one with the fake fruit tree base and shade fringed by dangling green grapes that rose up from the kitchen table. Della had for some reason thought lamps to be perfect works of art, and affordable, and she'd made a hobby of their collection, haunting flea markets and church sales searching for lamps, the older the better, even if she had to rewire them herself. One corner of the garage was cluttered with two dozen lamps of all types, most hopelessly broken, that she had meant to repair but never had.

The lamps that worked certainly did light the place up, but the white glow they cast also illuminated dust bunnies and cobwebs and the wilting jungle of plants that Stew hadn't taken much care of since early in the last winter, starting that day the ice storm pulled down the power lines and Della'd slumped over dead after bringing in firewood.

Stew's reddened eyes noted the spreading disorder of his house and he sniffed, for he'd become negligent as a widower. In prior years his domestic surroundings had always been clean and tidy, perfectly presentable in case visitors arrived at the drop of a hat.

He put on a pot of midnight coffee and thought about where to start. It seemed logical to begin with things living, so he went to the closet and found Della's plant waterer, a red plastic pitcher in the shape of a heron with a thin beak for a spout.

Stew filled the heron at the kitchen sink, staring at the dusty family pictures on the ledge above. There was one of himself and Della, her in a hugely brimmed white hat and swimsuit, him in long white pants and shirt, with a wide gaudy tie around his neck. That must've been taken up at Hot Springs just after they'd married, when he'd loved her completely, with no fineprint of doubts at all. The other pictures were of their children, Cynthia and Donald, and in each Cynthia stood apart, withdrawn, while Donald smiled broadly, his lips spread nearly from one jug ear to the other.

When the heron was full, Stew set it down and poured himself a cup of coffee. He let the cup sit, for he preferred his java lukewarm.

Oh, my, but just the thought of Johnny Shade made him feel sick about his life. And hers.

He picked the heron up and began to move, tending to the living things. He went into the front room and began the watering. Philodendron, dracaena, Boston ivy, begonia, jade plant—he knew the names but he didn't know which was which. Green things they were, unknown green growing things that overran their pots—the kind of crap Della had liked.

Stew sat on a stuffed footstool in the bright room, the pail in his hand, his head slumped.

She'd lied to him, he knew that. Hell-fire, there was no doubt about that at all. She'd lied to him and he'd let it pass, he'd let it pass from her sweet lips and into his own mind, where this single nasty falsehood had taken root and spread, growing like evil kudzu, growing over every thought he had of her, every casual comment she made to him, until whatever truths she may have told were hidden from him, overrun by his pitiful knowledge of her single lie.

He'd had her. That son of a bitch had known the smooth skin and sweet lips and strong hips of his wife.

And she'd lied about it.

And he'd let the lie take root around his heart, until real love had been choked off and died lonely.

Time to water the hanging plants now. There would be no sleep this night, and this house needed attention.

For nearly forty years Stew had loaded trucks at Bruns Van Lines, eventually becoming foreman. He had a knack for order, for keeping things straight, and as foreman these qualities proved to be worthwhile rather than merely prissy. To travel safely, truck cargo had to be packed precisely, the load balanced to avoid shifting and breakage, and he'd excelled at this. He'd sit in his tiny office off the loading dock, sketching the trailer and its dimensions down to the half-inch, then chart the cargo into place, each box or crate or tube destined for a precise position. The boys would do the work, surly boys most of the time, and he'd crab at them if they deviated at all from his design. Let's do it my way, he'd say, and despite a few curses they would. As the boys toiled and the trailer filled, each item in its place, the cargo filling the trailer to the roof in exactly the order he'd charted, he'd chew gum and beam and think to himself— Now I know why those ol' Pharoahs got so carried away!

To be a Pharoah in his personal life had been his desire, with every small or large domestic charm a building block to be stacked skyward toward a flesh-and-blood perfection, a monumental family harmony. But, no, if one key thing is out of place . . .

Monumental family harmony went unattained because of three words and a puppy, the puppy named Coral, the three words, "The bake sale." That was what she'd claimed, that's where she'd said she'd been. She baked terrific foods at home, but that's where she told him she'd been. She'd said it straight to his face, lying without any trace of effort, but her bag contained no bread, no pie, not even a single glazed donut, and because of Coral, their Beagle pup, the marriage was cracked, split wide, for Coral had slipped her leash and trotted off and he'd followed hollering for her, hollering up and down alleys and through vacant lots, the puppy lost to sight, and he'd come to the mouth of the alley down from Verdin's Grocery when he'd seen Della. He'd seen Della walking from behind the store, her hands held to her head, pinning her fragrant hair up, and he'd stood there watching, his throat dry from hollering and the whole terrible gamut of thoughts that immediately clutched at him, and he'd kept watching as she walked away, toward home, then Johnny Shade came from behind the store, in nearly the same footsteps as her, jauntily smoking a cigarette, but cunningly turning the opposite direction.

Stew had vomited against a fence, then gone off again after Coral. He couldn't find the pup in an hour so he'd gone home, and Coral was there already, with Della on the porch. "Where you been?" he asked. Della patted Coral and the puppy jumped up on her lap. "The bake sale."

After that he couldn't stop himself from asking that same question over and over, Where you been? Where you been? Where you been? If pretty Della went out to mail a letter, or get a quart of milk, or borrow sugar from Luann Nash next door, he asked the question by reflex on her return, without thought, Where you been? And of course she tired of this and began saying Where do you think I've been? and in years to come she either ignored the question altogether or came back flip, with some retort such as, Humpin' the Chinamen down at the laundry, or On a three-day toot with Frank Sinatra. He had tried to laugh sometimes, straining to find these comments funny, but more often he would suddenly become busy with the newspaper or start cleaning house, and say, Just curious is all.

Cynthia had been born the spring following the lie, and at first this had seemed a blessing, but the lie was loose in his mind now and not even a baby was safe from it.

These plants took more water than he had expected, so Stew went to the kitchen to refill the heron. While in there he knocked back a cup of coffee, then another. He intended to stay up all night cleaning. The time had come for it.

Just the thought of that man, that man and Della, and those three words of her answer, had ruined his marriage. Everything was affected.

He'd been a wrong father to Cynthia from the time her baby face began to take shape. She didn't look much like him, or Della, or any Lasseins or Rondeaus he'd ever seen. His uncle was blue-eyed, as was one of Della's brothers, but whenever he looked into Cynthia's big blues his chest would tighten. It was possible, just possible she was his, but by no means certain, and doubt is more evil than certainty, for a fact can be dealt with, got over, but doubt only feeds on itself and grows.

Donald was definitely his, for those jug ears and that goofy grin had stamped him as a Lassein more surely than a birth certificate. And Donald had been a happy kid— and why not, Stew had doted on him, giving him ninety-nine percent of his affections. Donald had grown up to be a confident sailor with a goofy grin, and was now a chief petty officer cruising the Indian Ocean.

Somehow Cynthia had known or felt his falseness with her. From babyhood she'd been shy, withdrawn, always watching, standing apart. He'd been gruff with her, never encouraging, and always short of temper. Several times he had spanked her too hard and once Della had smacked him for it. There had been tears shed in the dark over this, but he couldn't love her the same. Maybe not at all. When she was older she had told him his own feelings about her, right on the mark, in a ranting voice, saying he didn't love her, he never had, he only provided room and board.

She lived on the west side of St. Bruno now, in that sprawl of new streets and shopping centers out that way. Maybe three times a year he'd see her, and they'd have a drink and avoid the subject of their relationship, talking instead about new cars or gardening.

Stew set the water pitcher down and went to the phone. He dialed Cynthia's number, listening to the rings, hoping she'd answer rather than this beatnik what's-his-name she now lived with.

Like her mother before her, Cynthia had a weakness for shitheads. She married the first greasy rock 'n' roll shit-head who asked, and after that shithead caught on with a NASCAR pit crew and split to work the racing circuit Cynthia had moped a while, then moved in with Wilkie, a much older jazz-buff shithead who could pay her bar tab and roll a tight marijuana cigarette. This Wilkie fella worked in radio as a late-night mellow voice, and whenever they spoke he called Stew Big Daddy.

When the phone was answered it was Cynthia, so he didn't have to tolerate that Big Daddy business tonight.

"Hullo?" Her voice was whisky deepened, and he could hear Wilkie's radio voice in the background.

"It's me, honey."

"Who? Who is this?"

"Your daddy. Stew."

"Oh. Dad. Shee! Dad, it's two o'clock."

Stew looked at the clock on the wall and saw she was thirty minutes ahead of the truth.

"I'm cleanin' house," he said.

"At two in the mornin'?"

"That's right. Why I called is, do you know which of your mother's plants is which? I've been waterin' them, honey, but I don't know their names."

The sound of ice cubes clicking came over the line.

"Are you kiddin', Dad? You called for that?"

"Well, they're your mother's plants, and I noticed they're not doin' so hot. I'd like to know them by name. Maybe I should play music for them—they like that, don't they?"

"Yeah, they like that." Cynthia laughed and spoke to someone else. Whoever it was also laughed, probably at goofy ol' Big Daddy's expense. "Dad, I'll come over Sunday and tell you their names. I gotta go now—you get on to bed, hear?"

She hung up. He didn't blame her. Maybe he'd do some sweeping.

He brought the broom in from the back porch and carried it into the front room. The lamp lights had revealed all these cobwebs on the walls, so he raised the broom and batted at the webs. As he swung the broom he thought of Mister Snake-hips, Mister Crooner of Deceit, and swung harder. They'd been friends once, a slick double-play combo on the sandlots of Frogtown, but Johnny Shade became a self-loving sport who left ruins in his snake-hipped wake.

One New Year's Eve, when the kids were in high school, Della had sat up by herself drinking gin, listening to old music on the hi-fi, dancing by herself, even singing along in a loud voice with certain songs. When finally she came to bed he'd sat up and watched her undress in front of the window.

She fumbled with buttons, and stumbled.

Della, he'd said, are you happy?

Della had yawned, then sat on the edge of the bed.

What do you think? she asked.

He'd watched her back for a moment, then lay down and pulled the quilt up over his face.

Pennsylvania 6-5000.

# 8.

The kid was almost always up first of a morning, so she'd pour the whisky and take it to him. She'd wait until her father let rip with a series of hacking coughs that signaled his awareness of the new day, then fetch him a glass of Maker's Mark to slow the shaking of his hands. Those shakes of his were awful to see if he didn't get his angel of sour mash right away, and on those occasions when he tried to pour his own, he made embarrassing messes.

On this morning Etta had fixed her face in the bathroom mirror, getting fancy with her kit of cosmetics. She put on eye shadow of a brooding black hue to match the crucifix hanging from her ear. No one color seemed to be enough for her mouth, so she'd used dabs of them all to make rainbow lips. Her dark rat-tail tresses were fairly well combed out, and she'd brushed the femme-flattop part of her hair to perfect level.

While John X. sawed logs on the couch in the front room, she sat cross-legged on her cot in the kitchen, the pink Joan Jett suitcase on her lap. She had the lid up to provide secrecy, and behind it her hands held five thousand dollars in fifties that she was counting for the umpteenth time. Money that ran this high in amount had fabulous side effects, and as she snapped each bill onto the pile in the suitcase bottom her fingertips seemed to absorb greenback desires and rush them to her head. This much could buy: a CD player; one of those Ram-tough pick-up trucks; a cabin in Hawaii underneath a waterfall, like a cave, sort of, reached only by a secret bamboo ladder from below; an electric piano; a bass boat; a plane trip to Europe for her and Dad both.

But that last thing, the trip, was out. Mom had told her so, and told her so like she meant it. Randi Tripp, looking radiant in a sheer white dress, her black hair combed out and pulled back into a new look, had taken Etta by the hand and put the money into it. They were in the family Ford, pulled over to the curb near a highway ramp.

"He's your daddy," she'd said in a gust of peppermint breath, "and he cares for you, hon, but don't you *dare* let him know you have this money. Huh-uh. Under *no* circumstances. You keep it hid away, 'cause that's money for your college, baby."

Then Mom had put her out of the car and told her to walk from there to Enoch's Ribs and Lounge.

Etta closed the Joan Jett suitcase and slid it under the cot. She went to the window and stared out at the river, which was about the only hobby she had anymore. The wide brown flow surged south past the window and birds flew above it, high overhead.

Back home when her life had been regular she would be hearing songs by now. Possibly not whole songs but snatches for sure. Randi Tripp would be wandering about the trailer in her yellow robe working on her pipes, belting out a line or two about the way to San Jose, or little town blues, or impossible dreams the singer had. At any time of day Mom was likely to be singing, and if asked a question she frequently answered with a musical phrase.

If Etta wanted two dollars, the answer might be a growled, "Can't buy me love, oh, love, oh," etc.

Where's Dad? "Sooome-wheere, ov-er the rain-bow," etc.

On warm days Mom had liked to wash the Ford Escort on the little slab driveway next to the trailer. As soon as she came outside in her two-piece swimsuit, all the unemployed men in The Breeze-In Trailer Park, which was *all* of them but the one across the backyard, would rush out of doors to be handymen around their various trailers. The 'Bama Butterfly had a build on her that contributed greatly toward the general upkeep of the neighborhood, because she had a fetish about keeping that Escort spanking clean. She'd grab a big yellow sponge and squirt the hose and burst into song, turning the entire trailer park into a musical. She'd sponge the fenders clean and sing about the boogie-woogie bugle boy, or her and Bobby McGee, and when she rubbed the car down dry she shifted tempos and sang about strangers in the night, or whiter shades of pale. Once she had finished washing she would start rolling the hose up, and neighbor fellas would ask her to come over for iced tea, or beer, or champagne that'd been in the fridge since somebody's cousin's wedding. Randi Tripp never wanted any of what they offered, but she never was rude, she was nice, she smiled, she didn't step on their fantasies to the squashing point. No, she worked them like she would any other crowd, because to be a star they had to see you up there shining, so they could dream about you, but if they ever did reach up and actually touch a star and give it a squeeze, it'd just be revealed as a hot, hot rock and probably not worth a cover charge to see anymore.

That was the wonderful thing about Mom, Etta thought—she had her own fine opinion of herself and wasn't nobody could change it.

The twelve o'clock bells at St. Peter's had already sounded when John X. began coughing and harumphing into consciousness. Etta pulled the Maker's Mark down from the cupboard. She unscrewed the cap, then poured the whisky into a clear glass, filling it to the depth of four of her fingers. She raised the glass and smelled the sour mash and the scent caused her nose to wrinkle.

When Mom had been home she'd sometimes stop Etta from delivering these angels of whisky to John X. "You ain't a bartender, hon," she'd say. But Etta would listen to her daddy hacking in the other room and claim she didn't mind. Really. And, usually, after a few minutes more of hacks and groans, Mom would make a face like she'd broken another nail and say, "Oh, go on and coordinate your daddy, hon." Then Etta would take Daddy the whisky and his shaky hands would wrap around it, and not a word would be said until he'd drained the glass. Then he'd light a cigarette, and crack a joke that made her laugh, or tell a lie that interested her.

This morning on the river, in his son's house, was no different.

She carried the glass to his bed on the couch, and his hands trembled as he reached up and wrapped them around his morning angel of Maker's Mark.

John X. set the empty glass on the floor next to the couch. He patted his T-shirt where a cigarette pocket would hang on a button shirt, then grunted. On many mornings of late he could recall a ten-line conversation or a stolen kiss from back in 1949 in every detail, but could not find his cigarettes. He always seemed to be waking up in new spots for one thing, plus, those old acts and conversations came into his head so clearly that he sometimes wrung new meanings from them. Quite a few of the nuances and long silences that had baffled at the time now offered themselves up for interpretation in retrospect. They surely did. But that did not solve the real issue, which was, where'd I leave those smokes?

In this case the Chesterfields were discovered under the edge of the couch beside his eight-ball lighter and a full ashtray.

John X. lit one up, then grinned at Etta, who still stood there, just looking at him.

"Know why the crack in your butt goes long ways instead of sideways, kid?"

"So you don't go thump-thump-thump slidin' down stairs."

"Oh. I've told you that one, huh?"

"Mom did. She thought it was funny."

"I must've told it to her."

"Do you hate Mom?"

"Aw, please, no, kid. No, I don't really hate much of anything at all." John X. and his extremities were slowly pulling together. He was close to being together enough to stand and square up to yet another day. He looked at Etta with her thundercloud eye shadow and rainbow lips and said, "Ain't it about time for you to be in school, Etta?"

Etta sat on the arm of the couch.

"The school year hasn't started yet, Dad."

"It hasn't, huh?" John X. studied the burning end of his Chesterfield for a moment, then said, "I see these other kids with books and stuff—where're *they* goin'?"

"Oh, Dad," Etta said with a laugh. "Those kids go to Catholic schools, and I go to public."

"Uh-huh. When does public start? Seems like it used to start before the leaves all fell."

The black crucifix that hung from her ear was pinched between Etta's fingers, and she rubbed it.

"They don't make little kids chop cotton nowadays, Dad, so the school year is real different from when you went."

"Nah—they've all got machines now," he said. "So when *does* it start?"

"November," Etta said. She walked to the window and watched the endless flow of the big river. "I think ninth."

"Okay, then," John X. said. "November." He pulled his pants on without ever leaving the couch. "I'll see to it you're enrolled, kid. We got plenty of time." As he bent over to tie his black sneakers he saw the empty whisky glass. "School's a good thing for children," he said and lifted the glass. "Education." He held the glass above his head and tilted it to catch the bartender's eye. When he did, he grinned slightly, and said, "Another tiny angel, angel?"

When the workings of his body had come to seem totally familiar once more, John X. told Etta they'd grab a bite at The Catfish. He stuck his Balabushka cue under his left arm and told the kid that, while he wasn't precisely the Prince of Monaco, he figured he could finance a fish sandwich with a side of hush puppies.

Their walk through Frogtown to The Catfish Bar turned into a shambling guided tour, with John X. pausing to point out certain intersections or shacks or alleyways that he felt would be of special interest to his daughter. There was the corner he'd hung around starting at about her age; the alleyways he'd always preferred to open streets; the shack his boyhood best friend, Butter Racine, had lived in with his crazy old man, Crazy Racine, who was the first actual drug addict John X. could recall, with Butter becoming the second.

Etta's reactions to these points of interest were restrained, very low-key, and her audible response was either uh-huh or mm-hmm.

John X. called another halt near a busy corner that had a new gas station slash minimart on it.

"Right there," he said, pointing at the fuel pumps, "there didn't used to be a gas station. No, m'am. There used to be a little nite spot called Half-a-Heaven, with a sawdusted dance floor, and plenty of dark, moody corners."

"You liked to go there, Dad?"

"Oh, my yes," he said. "Everybody did. The whole world packed into that little joint on a good night." John X. lit a cigarette and stared at the gas station. He was still wearing clothes from a dead man's wardrobe, and though nothing fit quite right, somehow everything was comfortable. "Kid, let me tell you, women wore flowers in their hair in them days. To dances, bars, whatnot. Their hair would be long and hanging, but organized, you know, not running loose, and there'd be a big bright sweet flower of some sort planted in their hair. Just above the ear, usually, where a fella's face would nuzzle during a dance. They'd be red, or white, maybe yellow or pink—definitely sweet."

"Flowers?" Etta said. "I don't think that's cool anymore."

John X. looked down at Etta for a moment, then nodded once.

"Probably not," he said. "But it was not considered corny, then, kid, believe me."

They walked on down the sidewalk, and a minute later he added, "*Fetch*ing is more what it was considered."

The route to The Catfish led the old man and the kid past the intersection of Lafitte and Perry where Ma Blanqui's Pool House occupied the corner portion of a brick row house.

"That's where the mother of your brothers lives, kid."

"Are we goin' in?"

"Not today, kid. Let's get a move on."

As they walked past, Etta asked, "Did you do her like Mom done you?"

"I don't know. I guess. One mornin' I came to in Beaufort, South Carolina, and it was clear we'd drifted apart. I realized I was nowhere near done driftin', neither, and damn few wives can live with that."

"Mm-hmm. What's she like now?"

"She's an opinionated older woman, I imagine." John X. patted his daughter on the head so she'd follow him as he crossed the street. "Makes a mighty fine peach kuchen as I recall. Nice long hair to her shoulders. She raised your brothers up pretty decent."

The sign with the debauched blue catfish on it was now in sight.

"They seem sort of *rough*, Dad."

"Well," he said, shrugging.

"Tip cooks good coffee, though," Etta said.

"That's what I mean," John X. said.

John X. Shade, pool hustler in decline, was looking for a price on his Balabushka cue. Over the years he had hocked the cue perhaps twenty-five times, and on a few occasions left it temporarily in the custody of fellas who'd had his Number. He set the case on the bar of The Catfish and opened it. The cue lay in slots lined with green felt, and John X. rolled his hand along the fine pretty length of it. He rubbed his fingers over a slight score in the wood just below the ferrule that had already been there when he'd gotten the cue at a Johnson City Jamboree he'd played in back when his hands could form a firm bridge, and stroke smoothly, even brilliantly at times, and every honky-tonk or corner beer joint with an eight-foot table had represented a career opportunity.

"What'll you give me for this, son? You know what it's worth, don't you?"

Tip leaned over the counter from his side of the bar. He had a huge white apron on, and smelled strongly of after-shave.

"I know that stick is worth plenty to somebody who feels like payin' plenty for it," he said. "That person wouldn't be me, though."

"Why, hell," John X. said, "it's worth plenty to anybody with good sense. George Balabushka is dead, son, so this stick is like good earth as an investment—I mean, they won't be makin' any more of it."

This dickering with his own boy was not exactly fun, but fortunately there wasn't much of a crowd to see it. The lunch rush had passed. In the back two biker couples wearing Harley T's and tattoos lingered over their empty plates and full mugs to discuss the many traffic tickets they had earned but not paid, motorcycle maintenance, and similar domestic trivia. Three Catfish regulars, two of them older males, the other a squat, sulky woman in her thirties, sat nearer the door, each tippling at a separate table, though occasionally a few words were passed among them. Etta was down at the end of the bar sitting on a stool beside Tip's hippie chick, the kid eating hush puppies while Gretel read a tabloid.

Stew Lassein sat brooding over a beer glass two stools away from the girls. He was wearing white pants and a white shirt and a wide gaudy tie loose around his neck, appropriately duded up for an ice cream social that'd ended forty years ago. His normally pale skin was even paler, rinsed out, and he seemed in need of sleep.

That guy always was too square for this wicked round world, John X. thought. He actually liked Lawrence Welk and Kate Smith! And became a *foreman*, for cryin' out loud. He's now ending up exactly where the middle of the road leads you.

Let *that* sink in.

"This *is* a handsome thing," Tip said, looking at the cue. "I don't play much, or care to, but I can tell it's special." He lifted the butt from the case and hefted it. "Let me see you take a few shots with it, Johnny."

"No, no, now Christ, Tippy," John X. said, "I can't run six balls anymore. I might jaw out a hanger, even. It's terrible."

"Just shoot so I can see the stick in action before I put up money for it."

"Are you tryin' to embarrass me, boy? Is that it?"

Tip raised a hand to his long brown hair, flicked a stray strand behind his ear, then smoothed it back into greased formation. His face was down, as if studying the cue.

"Well, now, look," he said, "I'll hold this stick for you, Dad, and spot you fifty against it."

"Fifty?" John X. reached for the cue, then began to screw it together. The Balabushka had a blue twine grip, shiny brass fittings, and subtle cross-hatching on the lower shaft, but was otherwise austere and purposeful. "I need a hundred—maybe it'd help if you saw me run a few balls."

"I'll rack 'em," Tip said.

When John X. and Tip went toward the pool table, Gretel looked up from her reading. She'd been hip-deep into a story about a man in central Florida whose garden was attracting attention as a walk of fame because he had this weird knack for growing edibles, mainly potatoes and melons, that seemed to resemble certain movie stars, especially Curly from the Three Stooges and Shelley Winters, though he'd produced a far wider range of recognizably famous body parts, almost all of which were noses or breasts. There was a picture of a sweet potato that *did* sort of look like Curly, and the man held up two honeydews that had odd shapes for melons but perfect shapes for a starlet's breasts, and the man called them Marilyn. The man said the garden was a miracle, a pure gift, though the article seemed to poke some fun at him.

"Phooey," Gretel said. She then reached over and rubbed her hand across Etta's flattop, causing the hairs to bristle, and said, "I really do dig your hairstyle."

"My mom picked it," Etta said. "But I wear it."

"Don't you like it?"

Etta shrugged, nodded, shrugged again.

"I'm used to it," she said. She rolled another hush puppie through a puddle of tartar sauce, then popped it into her mouth. Gretel loomed over her, hugely pregnant in a red shift, her gray highland eyes looking resigned but alert. The scar on Gretel's cheek was fingernail wide, pink and mysterious, perhaps even romantic in origin. It started about an inch below the outside corner of her right eye, plowed a straight row at an angle across her cheek, and tailed off a fraction above the corner of her mouth. As Etta chewed the hush puppie she slowly raised her hand toward Gretel's cheek, stopping shy of contact. She swallowed hard. "How'd you get that scar?"

Gretel put the tips of four fingers lengthwise on the scar.

"Yah-weh hung it on me," she said somberly, "for not payin' attention. I was s'posed to be steerin'."

"Yah-who?" Etta asked.

"Yah-weh. That's God in other places."

"Could I touch it?" Etta asked. "I'll take care not to scratch."

Gretel pulled her fingertips from the scar and raked back her blond hair.

"Help yourself," she said. "It's different."

Oh so lightly Etta touched her fingers to the scar, then slid them along the track of proud flesh. Her young face and bright eyes reflected her enthrallment.

"Wow," she said. "Holy freakin' wow! It's slick, ain't it? Slick like satin."

Laughing softly, Gretel leaned her face down to Etta's touch.

"I've come to love the feel of it," she said. "Spiritually, it's quite a reminder."

"It's slick like satin," Etta said again. Then: "Say, could I rub your butterfly, too?"

"Sure," Gretel said. "The Monarch just feels like skin, though."

In a gruff, tired tone, Stew leaned toward Gretel and said, "Tell me about it. Tell me about scars from not payin' attention. I got mine that very same way."

Gretel smiled at him, and Etta said, "Where is it?"

"What?"

"Your scar."

Stew held a hand to his chest, then tapped a finger over his heart.

"Uh-huh," Etta said. "That scar is what set you cryin' last night."

Stew said, "Your daddy doesn't love you, li'l girl. I feel I have to tell you that. Your daddy doesn't love nobody he don't see in the mirror when he shaves."

"Now that is harsh talk, mister," Gretel said. "You hush up."

"Li'l girl needs to know," Stew said. He was avoiding eye contact. "Things need to be brought out, you see."

"Hush up."

"It's for the good of all."

"Mom used to say the same thing," Etta said.

"Listen to your mom, li'l girl."

"I didn't believe her, neither."

"What do you call love anyhow?" Gretel asked. "Answer me that, mister, then I'll hear you out. But if you can't answer me that, you should hush up."

The trio fell silent at this, and went back to their individual contemplations: Gretel, the tabloid; Stew, the past; Etta, the number of faces in Dad's mirror.

Down toward the rear of the room, at the one pool table, John X. stood slouching with the cue in his hands, watching as a simple cut-shot on the nine missed the corner pocket by a full inch.

"Over-cut," he said. He lined up a cross-table bank on the three ball, and stroked it toward the side-pocket, but it went wide and skidded down-table. "Are these rails soft?"

"Maybe," Tip said. "That could be it."

John X. made two hangers in a row, though his stroke was shaky even on them.

"More like it," he said. Then he leaned over the table, his eyes watering, bridge wavering, and missed six straight puppy shots, not even slopping one in. "What'd I tell you, son?" He began to unscrew the cue as he led the way back to the bar. At the bar he put the cue in the case and snapped it shut. "Terrible. Fuckin' terrible. I'm cursed. The pool god hates me, and that's a spiteful, petty son-of-a-bitch when he hates you. I told you it was terrible."

Tip set the cue under the bar.

"You didn't lie," he said. "You told it like it was."

John X. rattled the ice in his glass.

"I'm cursed," he said. "I should've got a job forty years ago. Maybe fifty. That's right. A *job*. But I thought, Work? The only things that like *work* are donkeys, and they turn their ass to it. Where's the future in work when I could use that stick, there, and hold the table for three-four hours at a whack—know what I'm tryin' to say, Tippy?"

"Sure. You're cursed."

"Nail on the head, son."

Tip went to the register and slapped together some fives and tens, then spread the money on the bar.

"There you go," he said to John X. "And, Johnny, I ain't your mother or nothin', but you think maybe you should eat something?"

"Might be I'll eat a peach later," John X. said jauntily. He scooped up all the money but a twenty. He put the roll in his pocket, then waved the twenty overhead, swishing the bill through the air before slapping it on the bar. "Refreshments for all, Tippy! Set everybody up. Get those gorgeous gals at the end of the bar another of whatever they're drinkin', and give ol' Stew, there, a nice libation on me."

Stew snorted derisively.

"I don't want a lie-bation on you," he said.

John X. sidled down the bar toward Stew, but left a few feet of polished bar rail between them. He tapped out a smoke and fired up. "Somethin' wrong with my money, Stewart?"

"Don't call me Stewart. It's insulting the way you say it."

"That beer in front of you looks dead, Stew," John

X. said with a shrug. "Hey, Tip, a couple of live whiskies over here."

Bent over the broad surface of the bar, with his white attire, white hair, and pale skin, his thin lips curled back from a mouthful of bright expensive teeth, Stew had the appearance of a truculent ghost. A ghost with a grudge.

"I won't take a drink bought with bad money," he said.

Tip set the drinks in front of the two old men, his head bent to hear their conversation.

"Now how can money be bad?" John X. asked. He spit on his hands, then ran his fingers through his wavy hair. "If it spends, it spends."

"This'll spend," Tip said, and picked up the twenty.

Stew snatched his drink aloft and dumped it to the floor.

"If money ain't worked for," he said, "then it ain't good."

The whisky made a puddle on the rough wood of the floor. John X. tapped the toes of his black sneakers in the puddle.

"Criminentlies," he said as he smeared the whisky underfoot, "that was a buck and a half, Stew. This ain't VJ Day anymore, slick. Drinks ain't a quarter no more, with a beer back and a pig's foot thrown in free."

"Your money is bad money," Stew said. "Which is the only breed of money a bad man spends."

"How bad a man am I if I'm buyin' you a drink?"

"There's guilt in you, Johnny."

"I think I'll pause to let *that* sink in, slick."

The bar was made of dark sturdy wood, and behind it there was a narrow passage backed by a small mirror, and a three-tiered display of liquor bottles. Sunlight came through the front windows and glinted off the bottles and the mirror.

"I *can* say I never *wanted* to be a bad fella," John X. said. He lifted his drink and held the whisky to his nose, inhaling the scent. "But, I've got to admit, sometimes opportunity was in such a lenient position I couldn't turn my back to it."

"I have it in mind to break your face," Stew said. He made no move, but stayed hunched over, talking into his glass of dead beer. "You always was Mister *So*-handsome—like there wasn't a man on earth handsomer'n you."

"Well, now, I always figured any man better lookin' than me was just a li'l *too* pretty—know what I mean? Like, say, Tyrone Power."

"And a funny talker, too," Stew said. "I never liked that about you neither. It's somethin' girls work at. I never liked it in you. Another reason to break your face. That makes two."

"Do you need more?" John X. asked. He tossed his drink back, and swiveled to face Stew. "Maybe I could tell you some more, slick, if you have this terrible need to add 'em up."

"I know your whole story," Stew said. "You used to screw about every third girl over ten years old in this neighborhood. Tell 'em lies, or true things they dream of hearin', then whisk their li'l cotton panties to their knees."

"Jealous?" John X. asked. He glanced toward Etta. "That's horseshit, anyhow." He smiled at Stew. "It's horseshit I actually wish was true—I could think back on such events and grin."

"Monique wasn't but about twelve when you married her, you rat."

"Rat? You better watch it. And she was *fourteen*—there's a difference."

"That's three," Stew said, then spun from his stool, and belted John X. with the bitter haymaker he'd been wanting to land ever since Coral the Beagle slipped her leash. This sucker punch landed on the button, and John X. was propelled from his stool and onto his ass.

John X. wobbled up from the floor, his eyes fixed on Stew. He spit theatrically, then raised his shaky old dukes.

"Why you sissy," he said. "I'll whup you 'til you pooch."

"Hah!" Stew barked. He then reached to his mouth and pulled his dentures out. He set them beside his beer. "Awl bwek oo flace!"

"Hey, hey," Tip said. He'd been pouring sodas for the ladies but now he rushed up the bar. "What is this shit, Johnny?"

John X. shot a pretty left jab plunk onto Stew's nose.

"Dinn hur!" Stew blurted, without the usual translation that dentures made. "Midda Wo-ansom!"

One of the bikers in the back laughed, then said, "Scope the old scrappers!"

Etta and Gretel got off their stools and stood watching the fracas, holding hands.

John X., in his comfortable suit of dead man's clothes, circled left, dukes held high, while Stew, in his apparitional attire, planted his feet and looked to land a bomb. John X. tried another jab but was short by a foot, and Stew lunged forward, his wild swing missing totally, but the two old noggins collided. Both men turned away, rubbing at their foreheads while making grunts of pain.

Tip wiped his hands on his apron and said, "Get him, Johnny. Kick his ass."

Stew recovered first and banged a right to John X.'s shoulder. John X. winced, then began to bounce on his toes, attempting lateral movement, but all the bouncing caused him some dizziness and he appeared ready to swoon.

"I got another reason for you," he said angrily. "Della told me I danced better'n you!"

"Huh-uh!"

"Oh, yeah, she did—at the Half-a-Heaven."

"Huh-uh!"

"On a slow dance, too."

Stew moved forward, his gnarled fists clenched and held low to his sides, and John X. stuck another jab to his beak, drawing blood, but Stew's low fists hooked to the belly, and John X. landed on his ass again, looking up.

Darting quickly to the bar, Stew reinserted his dentures so his insult would be intelligible. "That's the power of a *man*!" he said, then slipped the dentures out again and set them on the bar.

"Man?" John X. muttered as he stood. "Why, you're just a *baby* fartin' around in a *man's* suit. You always was, Stew."

Though his aching ribs caused him to hunch forward somewhat, John X. was slightly bouncing again, attempting to employ the tactical stragedy of Billy Conn, his idol of yore. He slid left to right and back again, then pumped out a double jab, landing one on Stew's upper lip and nose. Blood spots began to appear on the shirtfront of Stew's apparitional attire, but suddenly John X. grimaced and crouched to one knee, from which position he vomited onto the brass foot rail of the bar.

Gretel and Etta had stood watching the old men fight, Etta rubbing her flattop nervously, Gretel massaging her pregnant hump. Now Etta pulled her hand free of Gretel and ran to John X. Instant tears appeared on her face.

"Dad!" She flung herself on John X. from behind, her arms around his neck. "Dad!"

Gretel said, "Can I stop this? Can I put a stop to this?" She approached Stew. "Aren't you ashamed?" she said to his face. "You're bleedin' bad—what's violence settle, anyhow?"

Some sort of retort came from Stew, but the words were mysterious and weakly offered.

"Fight! Fight! Fight!" the biker couples chanted.

"Here, Gretel," Tip said, and handed her some napkins.

Gretel took the napkins and began to swab Stew's bloody nose. He stood there and let her, making weird humming sounds as her fingers wiped his nose and lips of blood.

After a moment he pulled away from her. His eyes were wild and red. He slid his teeth back into place, his hands trembling and his breath shallow. He looked toward the door and shook his head.

"Oh, I don't know!" he said. "I don't know still!"

Then he walked past John X., to the door, and out.

When the door closed the ladies helped John X. up, then sat him on a stool. Etta clung to him while Gretel took a napkin to the vomit around his mouth.

"Maker's Mark," he said. "A double."

This entire event seemed to strike Tip as humorous, and as he set the drink before his father, he said, "As a dad maybe you have been a pretty sorry deal, but as an ol' fucker to get drunk with and have around, Johnny, you're a fistful of fun. Know it?"

"I'm touched," John X. said.

"What's his problem with your face, anyhow? I couldn't catch his drift about that."

After a soothing sip, John X. said, "See, son, in years gone by I always was your basic average citizen of the type who should've been arrested but only once in a while was. Folks of a certain sort *will* hold that against a man. I guess I did this, I did that, and now and again some other thing altogether. I wore flashy clothes for Frogtown, and my pockets didn't have no fishhooks in 'em, and the neighborhood girls liked that about me. And maybe not too many mirrors cracked when I looked in 'em, and I think girls liked that, too. Flashy clothes, no fishhooks in my pockets, and bein' a dreamboat were things quite a few fellas *did not* care for about me, but girls did, and girls that liked me, well, as a rule, I found things I liked about them, too. A nice shape, or lovely hair of any hue, brown eyes, blue eyes, green eyes, a wet voice, a cute gap in their front teeth—if they liked my style I liked theirs. Stew, for one, never could stand me for my bigheartedness."

"Long time to hold a grudge," Tip said.

John X. turned on his stool, and the ladies were standing close by. He stroked Etta's hair, while looking into Gretel's face.

"That scar is hard to get out of my mind," he said. "It makes you look like a woman of intrigue, a visitor from faraway places."

Gretel grinned and shuffled her feet.

"I wish," she said.

John X. raised his glass in salute.

"To you two gorgeous kids," he said, then tossed back

the whisky. He stood and started walking toward the door, Etta hanging onto his coattail. He pulled the door back and stood in the opening. He looked out onto Lafitte Street, then up at the bright hot sun. "It may be that all I ever did with my life was to the bad, but, damn, son, I sure would like to do it all again."

# 9.

As he'd driven up from the coast and through the night, Lunch Pumphrey had trusted totally to the map of geography retained in his memory, and thus ended up well away from his destination. The atlas in his mind had gotten foggy at the 'Bama border, but not scarily so, and he'd plunged on into the dark night only to finally find himself in an actual place that wasn't on his map at all. No way could he reconcile himself to this lost position. He hadn't seen any sign whatever of Memphis, and he was positive he had to pass through there before he hit the Big River. Or, if not Memphis, certainly Arkansas, or some such southern state whose name he'd blanked on entirely, but that would still be there to pass beneath his wheels anyhow. Yet Memphis had not appeared, nor had any expected state name known or blanked.

Early in the A.M., with merely a clouded moon above, Lunch admitted his lostness to himself and took to studying road signs so intensely that the Bug faded off the blacktop, through a ditch, then into a billboard that said See Rock City. The right headlight was blinked. Metal had screamed from the fender and rolled down to bog the front tire, which had been cut open and hissed angrily for a moment.

Lunch leaned his unhurt head to the steering wheel, and his lips kissed the horn.

"I'm sorry," he said.

It was very early in a new day but Lunch was already on Salem number three before he'd found a farmhouse and called a tow truck. The wrecker hauled the Bug into a place called Natchez, and Lunch found himself stuck there until Virgil or Bill, the head grease monkeys, could get around to fulfilling his mechanical needs.

As the sun rose Lunch learned that he had found the river, at least, and the town itself was one of those places that bubbled over with history. For a while Lunch stood around in Virgil and Bill's station, but there were others milling around there, too, which meant he had a long wait coming to him. So he set his snap-brim hat atop his head at a rakish angle and went for a stroll along a sidewalk on a bluff that overlooked the huge brown water.

The bluff was grassy, with rock-walled flower beds, and fallen leaves seemed to be picked up as they fell, for there were only a few on the ground. The day was weirdly hot. It should have been jacket weather, but it was bare skin weather, and Lunch sweated in his all-black attire. A kindly woman gave him one of the leaflets she'd been fanning her face with, and he found a park bench to squat on while he read it.

Before reading the leaflet he opened his eyes to the wide view of the river and let himself absorb the wonder of it. Only those immigrants who dive for sponges, or a South Seas type of person, could swim across it. The water was that wide, the current that strong. A shitload of birds flew above this majestic landmark, and a barge floated on it. Lunch felt that he might possibly come to where he could care for a body of water like that. Especially when these birds are strung all along above it, and others fill the trees on the banks, which makes our feathery friends seem like they are an audience swooping to take seats at an upcoming event of a pleasing sort.

"That's a river, ain't it?" a man's voice said.

A man and woman in their thirties sat on the next bench. They'd been at Virgil and Bill's also.

"Good view," Lunch said.

The leaflet was on blue paper, and he picked it up to read. The whole thing concerned Natchez and the Natchez Trace. There were suggestions on where to go, where to eat, where to sleep, what times the seven-dollar horse-drawn carriages took off, and what special spots they trotted past. The few lines about history had a section that stood out, and Lunch read it twice: "John Thompson Hare, the hoodlum, was among the first who shrewdly saw the possibilities of banditry on the Trace. The Trace made him rich, but moody. In its wilderness he went to pieces, saw visions, was captured, and hanged."

"Damn," Lunch said. "This place makes you think."

The man on the next bench said, "It's got a bizarre history that's awfully attractive."

"Our forefathers," Lunch said, "were a rugged bunch."

"Oh, yeah, buddy," the man said. "The dudes down here in historical days were truly some rough cobs. No doubt about it."

"Some of it's sad, too," Lunch said.

He stood and approached the couple and held his hand out to the man, who was large. They shook, then Lunch extended his hand to the woman, who was knitting away at a ball of red yarn. She took his hand and slightly over-held it.

"Rich Moody," Lunch said, "pleased to meet you."

"Our name is Smith," the man said, then the woman said, "John and Mary Smith," then they both said, "and we ain't kiddin'!" This bit was well rehearsed, and the Smiths giggled at the end.

"That's cute," Lunch said.

"Thanks," said John Smith. "We hail from corn country, north of Cedar Rapids, south of Waterloo."

"Uh-huh. I saw you at Virgil and Bill's."

"That's right. We saw you there, too. Is that bruise on your face from your wreck?"

Lunch touched his fingers to his face.

"Oh, yeah," he said.

"We were in one, too," Mary said. "We got blind-sided by a local resident."

"That's true," John Smith said. "We've been on vacation, but, as it turns out, we've made money on the whole deal." He inclined his large form toward Lunch. "The other driver was tipsy, see, but well-to-do, and her family paid off in cash an hour ago."

Mary reached into her handbag and held up a flat thick booklet of money.

"This'll spend," she said, and her husband went "Hee-hee."

At this moment Lunch decided to scrutinize John and Mary Smith.

John Smith had the complete barnyard of personal characteristics: ox-sized, goose-necked, cow-eyed, a hog gut, probably mule-headed, and clearly goaty of appetite. His hair was black and worn in the style of an early Beatle. He sported a thin decadent mustache that suggested he just might have a few perversions he wouldn't *insist* on keeping private. Possibly John Smith would pass for kinda cute at an I-80 truckstop.

The distaff half of the Smiths from corn country acted meek but talked from the side of her mouth. Her fingers were diligent, clicking those needles, knitting something red that would surely be warm. Her hair was the color Ray-anne's had been, the color of corn ready for harvest, not too long, pulled back into a ponytail. Mary Smith's hips were thin, maybe even skinny, but somehow her breasts were huge presences behind a white T-shirt that advertised The Old Creamery Theater.

"This heat," Lunch said. "Whew! Could I interest y'all in somethin' cool to drink?"

Mary looked up at him and smiled, then turned to her husband.

"I *love* the way they talk down here."

"I know it," John Smith said. Then, to Lunch, "Hell, yes, little buddy, lead the way."

"That's a problem," Lunch said. "I just got here. I don't know the way."

"Oh, well," John Smith said, "we've been here two days, so we'll think of a spot."

"The saloon," Mary said, still knitting. "The old one under the hill."

Lunch pulled a wad of cash from his pocket.

"I'll get the first round," he said.

John Smith clapped his hands together.

"By golly, it looks like you can afford to," he said. He patted Lunch on the shoulder. "Follow us, little buddy."

The Smiths walked Lunch to Natchez Under-the-Hill. They pointed out several antique houses and lampposts that dated from the era when the town was jammed with river men, whores, bandits, slumming gentry, and assorted frontier ruffians. It was the memory of those lively times that prompted tourists to come here and gawk at surviving reminders of that rough-and-ready past.

The tavern they chose was called the Under-the-Hill, and it had been opened originally back when the very term Under-the-Hill meant buckets of grog, long knives, loose women, expansionist dreams, and sudden endings. The walls did seem to give off some faint echoes from key events in the lives of people who'd been dead a century or more.

The threesome sat at a table near a window, the river in easy view.

"We were here yesterday," John Smith said. "What're you drinking, Rich?"

"I'm a Bud man," he said, "and a Cub fan."

"He knows our motto!" Mary exclaimed, not addressing Lunch directly.

"I heard it," said John Smith. "Everybody back home is a Cub fan—I didn't know they were down here."

"Cable," Lunch said. "When Harry Caray says somethin', he speaks for me, too."

"Grrr-eat," said Mary. "I think I'll have a Bud with you guys."

Over three bottles of beer Lunch got the story of John and Mary Smith's lives, which were, though dull in the telling, extremely detailed. The details were relentlessly tacked on to the main body of the dull narrative, and there were several sidetracks in the tale where the Smiths took shots at each other over minor domestic disputes. He didn't pick up his socks, or do dishes, or cook anything but red-hot chili and spareribs, while she irked him by buying cheap beer instead of good beer, letting her sister visit for up to six weeks at a time, and by singing Patsy Cline songs in such a horrible manner that they were ruined for him as tunes, even when Patsy herself sang them. Late in the tale Lunch found himself appointed as the final judge in a wrangle that the Smiths had kept going for most of their marriage, to wit: should coffee be electro-perked and taken black so it tasted like *coffee* (him), or dripped and taken with milk to avoid throat cancer (her).

Three beers and no sleep had Lunch ready to feel like a judge, and he ruled on the coffee case by saying, "Electro-perk it, and serve it black, but make sure he gets ten minutes or more of titty-suck per diem, and that should make things *just* all around."

For a moment the only sound was knitting needles clicking. Then Mary looked directly at Lunch for a change. Her eyes were green and hot on him. She said, "That is an interesting answer. Black coffee and titty-suck—we never thought of it, but it's good."

John Smith had his head tilted back, and a lopsided smile put a kink in his mustache.

"Hee, hee," he went. "She's got the titties for it, doesn't she?"

Lunch glided his beer bottle along the wet spots on the table.

"No gentleman would answer that question," he said. "But she damned sure does."

Mary laughed and said, "He's the *cutest* little man."

John Smith again made the noise of "Hee, hee, hee." Then he said, "Let's us all go for a carriage ride—what say?"

They caught a carriage on Canal Street. Lunch and the Smiths spread across the seat, with Mary in the middle, still knitting. The carriage was open to the air and hot sun, pulled by a dark horse that didn't seem anxious for the work. The driver, a pudgy young man in regular modern clothes, except for a funky period hat, called out the landmarks and special memories of the town in a loud voice and tended to get a mite hysterical about old-timey architecture and certain ancient bloody deeds.

Lunch found the ancient bloody deeds to be especially interesting. The Natchez Trace had been nicknamed the Devil's Backbone, which was a phrase so strong it belonged in a song, perhaps as the chorus. The Devil's Backbone had been run all up and down by bottom-born, forceful types of fellas who Lunch wouldn't've minded drinkin' a few Buds with. Their criminal actions, and the still remembered drama of their bloody lives, spooked feelings awake and made them flit about in Lunch's deeper parts.

The carriage rattled past this old house and that old house, all of them with the proper names of people, and the horse and driver cut around pick-up trucks hauling pumpkins, RVs of the retired, and Japanese automobiles. Only Mary really liked the house stuff (this was the Smiths' third carriage ride in two days), while Lunch and John Smith both studiously blotted their minds with the historical gore and all its fine points.

When the carriage ride ended the trio went into a tavern called Mike Fink's. Mike Fink was another riverfront legend, one who had apparently talked a whole lot of boastful trash that had been passed down. His daddy was an alligator, his mammy was a hurricane, he ate gunpowder for breakfast, and whipped whole armies with his farts, and so on. Several of his allegations in this vein had been painted on weathered boards and tacked to the walls.

Lunch and the Smiths stuck to Bud, with the addition of burgers, the Smiths buying, since, as it now came out, they had thirty-six hundred dollars on them.

Though she didn't seem to look at him much, Mary made some observations about Lunch. For one thing, she said the bruise on his face looked older than from last night. Lunch answered by saying the human body is a funny piece of work. A while after that she pointed a knitting needle at his feet, then his hands.

"He has the itsy-bitsiest hands and feet—have you noticed?"

John Smith made that hee, hee, hee sound again, which was becoming an irritant.

"Haw, haw, haw," Lunch said, as an antidote.

"Well you *are* small, little buddy," John Smith said. "Like Little Harpe, who was the brother of Big Harpe, who as brothers murdered and robbed countless travelers along the Devil's Backbone. I've read up on it."

"Little and Big who?"

"Harpe," John Smith said. "One was known as Little and the other as Big, and the different gangs along the Devil's Backbone considered both the Harpes to be beyond the pale, just too darn strange in their crimes. There was a freaked-out style to the way they murdered and carried on that shook these other murderers up to where they avoided Little and Big as much as possible."

The thing Mary was knitting had begun to take shape as a sturdy knee-sock. From the side of her mouth she said, "Tell him about the baby, and the bodies."

"The Harpes had some women with them, little buddy, and naturally they ended up with kids. But Big was real uptight, and when a baby, his *own* baby, mind you, bothered him by squalling and keeping everybody awake, why, Big snatched the baby up by its heels and smashed its head against a tree trunk."

"No shit?" Lunch said. He was listening raptly, as if to his own family history. "What'd Little do?"

"I think they all went to sleep," John Smith said. "The squalling was over. Their great talent, though, was the disappearance of bodies. The folks they murdered didn't get found very often. See, the Harpes were farm boys, mean farm boys, and they'd learned some things slaughtering animals back home. You take a body of a person, hee, hee, hee, and you split it through the gut, the tummy, scoop out the innards and toss in rocks, see, then kick it in the river. It won't come up. The gas escapes through the split as the victim rots, instead of ballooning up, and with the rocks in the tummy, it just sits in the riverbed and bottom-feedin' fish nibble away all evidence of the crime."

"Gee," Lunch said. "History is really okay."

"History was always my best subject," John Smith said.

"Mine was recess."

"I guess that's why I'm tellin' this, and you're hearin' it."

"I guess." Lunch checked the clock on the wall. "Those sure were wild times."

"That they were, little buddy," John Smith said. "I must say I think it'd've been a real adventure to be down here in those days. I really do. I expect I could've handled myself among that sort pretty well. I've got the size, plus, I can *fight* if I got to."

Mary said, "You ain't been in a fight since you smacked Alice Buchtel's boy for throwin' a snowball at your Caprice."

"But in *those* days, hon, I would've had to be in them all the time, which would improve my hand-to-hand skills. I *can* fight when I have to. And when I've *had* to I've ended up on top as a rule."

"Oooh," Lunch said. "I can't imagine such violence. A little fella like me, why, it wouldn't do for me to mix in violence like that."

Mary said, "You know his tiny boots look like they'd fit *me*."

"Please don't wrestle me down and take my clothes from me, m'am. Especially my boots."

"He's cute. He's the *cutest* little man."

When the trio had finished their burgers and Buds, Lunch wowed them by showing off his left forearm tattoo that read Cubs Win! They gushed about that for a moment, then Lunch said he had to go check on the status of his Bug at Virgil and Bill's. The Smiths needed an update on their Caprice, so they all walked to the station together.


Neither Virgil or Bill wore name tags, but for some reason Lunch thought it was Virgil he talked to. This possible

Virgil said that Lunch had lucked out, and at a nearby car cemetery they'd found a fender for the Bug, though it was a flat black color. A new tire had been slapped on, balanced, and aligned. The dents in the front bonnet had been pinged out fairly well, but not perfectly.

"I'll see to that myself," Lunch said. "What do I owe you?"

With the tow charge, the tire, the fender, the labor, and the inscrutable miscellaneous, the total bill was equal to the take from three convenience-store robberies. But the immediate future seemed so rich in prospects that Lunch paid up without any complaint.

The deal on the Smiths' Caprice was less certain. It was set to roll as soon as a side door was put on, but the side door was on order from Vicksburg and late in arriving.

"This lazy ol' river has slowed these people down," Mary said. "I want to go back to the room and get some rest. My eyes hurt."

"I hate to see good folks like you turn spiteful on the region," Lunch said. "Folks down here are nice as pie. I mean, the sun'll set in two hours, and my car is runnin'. How's about I carry y'all to dinner in the country? A mom-and-pop place out at the crossroads. The moon'll be on the water."

"Well," John Smith said. He looked at Mary, who nodded. "It's a date, but only if you let us pay, okay?"

Lunch waited mostly on a park bench for the sun to set. He did some scurrying around the grounds. A snort of cocaine added flaky clarity to his thoughts. For amusement he had the river and the birds in view. Pretty soon he needed to push on to St. Bruno, which he'd learned was an easy drive away. But first, dinner with the Smiths from corn country. When it was dark he went into action.

He drove the Bug at a slow speed toward The Cromworth Motel, where the Smiths had a room. Their room was off the road, and as he cruised back that way he saw them, standing in front of room one eleven, both holding pink wine coolers, staring at the small swimming pool in the courtyard.

Lunch parked a foot short of their kneecaps. He leaned his head, hat and all, out the window.

"Howdy, howdy," he said. "Feelin' hungry?"

"Famished," Mary Smith said. She had her blond hair fanned out around her face, and she wore a short red cocktail dress that showed her fit, firm gams on one end, and a mile of creamy cleavage on the other. "I could eat your black hat with ketchup."

"We can do better'n that," Lunch said. He kept the clutch put in and revved the Bug engine. "This mom-and-pop place Virgil told me about *special*-izes in catfish and chicken."

"Big platters, I hope," John Smith said as he opened the passenger door.

"They serve family style," Lunch said. "You'll get your gut stuffed alright."

"Hee, hee, hee."

The Smiths tossed their wine coolers into a trash can, then climbed into the Bug. Because of his size John Smith crawled into the back seat, which he needed all of. Mary rode shotgun, her large bag of knitting resting on her lap.

"In case I get bored," she said, tapping the bag.

"You won't," Lunch said.

Lunch pulled away from The Cromworth Motel. At the main drag he guessed south. Streetlights and assorted neon lit the way, and Lunch drove slowly through sparse traffic.

"This thing seems to be luggin'," John Smith said.

"All this weight," Lunch said.

At the edge of town Lunch kept going. There were still pockets of houses along the way on one side of the road. A big yellow harvest moon was hung in the sky, casting a terrific golden glow that seemed peculiarly invented, perhaps by some lone nut spiritual figure, or else rigged up by Hollywood technicians to bathe a love story in. Once in a while the river burst into view between rows of trees, the brown water golden in the night.

"Are we lost yet?" Mary asked.

"It's a little further out this way," Lunch said. He saw a gravel lane in the high beams, a lane that turned toward the water. "I think this could be it."

He turned off the paved road and onto the gravel.

"It sure is dark," John Smith said.

"Dark enough?" Mary asked.

"Yup."

She reached into her knitting bag and raised out a nickel-plated revolver. She pulled back the hammer and put the barrel at Lunch's head.

"If you want to stay cute, li'l man," she said in a jailhouse tone, "you'll stop when I tell you to."

"What the hell is this?" Lunch said.

"Banditry," John Smith said. "Hee, hee, hee."

He leaned forward from the rear seat and touched a hunting knife blade to the side of Lunch's throat. "Welcome to the Devil's Backbone, you redneck punk."

The lane abruptly ended at the river's edge. High beams from the Bug shone way out across the water.

"Stop," Mary said. "Or I'll bust a cap in your fuckin' face."

"Hey, now," Lunch said as he braked. "Don't shoot me, Mary. Please. I'm a harmless tiny fella."

"You are now," John Smith said. "Where'd you do your time?"

"What time is that?"

"Oh, cut the comedy," Mary said. "You're a jail-bird if we ever seen one—were you fixin' to rob us?" She leaned across and tapped the pistol barrel to his bruised cheek. "You cute tiny man—did you figure you could take *us* off?"

"Hee, hee, hee."

"Leave the lights on," Mary said. "And get your ass out that door. You run and I'll drill you."

"She can do it, Rich," John Smith said. "I've seen her."

"Y'all ain't from Iowa," Lunch said. He kept both hands firmly on the steering wheel. "Corn country don't behave like this."

"The hell it don't," John Smith said. "Hee, hee, hee. You need to travel more."

All three of them got out of the Bug.

"Stand in the light," Mary said. "And toss that big wad of cash you got tucked in your pocket on the ground there, Rich."

As Lunch emptied his pocket of cash, John Smith kicked at the gravel, spraying tiny rocks about.

"This stuff is too small," he said sadly.

Mary came into the light, her red dress brilliant in the

glow, shiny pistol glinting, her blond hair gleaming like Rayanne's used to do when she'd just finished washing it.

"One thing," she said, "would you say our skit worked, Rich?"

"Skit?"

"The knitting, Rich. The knitting and the corn country yucks—did it make us come across as lovey-dovey hicks, ripe for pluckin'?"

"Totally took *me* in," Lunch said.

John Smith grabbed the pistol from Mary, then they kissed briefly.

"We just love the outlaw life," he said, waving the pistol. He did a little dance on the gravel, his large body bouncing. "The way we live it, it could go on forever."

"There aren't too many couples like us, Tiny Baby," Mary said. "We're gonna make this romance last."

"There it is, Gina," Tiny Baby said. "Shared interests bind."

"Your names ain't John and Mary Smith neither, huh?"

"Not exactly."

"This is devastatin'," Lunch said. "I'll never fully trust a blond slut and a big fat slob again."

Tiny Baby said, "I doubt you'll be meetin' any more, Rich." He smacked the black hat from Lunch's head, then shoved Lunch toward the river. "I'll bet that water's *just right*."

When Lunch was shoved again he fell, and while down he slid the derringer from his boot.

"I'm scared," he said. "I'd like to pray." And as Tiny Baby swaggered toward him, smirking, he raised the derringer and shot the big man, catching him in the throat.

Tiny Baby staggered back into the light, blood spraying from his neck. The pistol fell from his hands, and he sunk to his knees. Lunch said, "Crawl, you dirty dog!"

Tiny Baby gurgled blood, wheezing on his knees, his head bowed to the ground.

"Well, I got a heart," Lunch said.

Then he put the derringer at Tiny Baby's temple and pulled the trigger. The big man dropped, face down in the gravel.

Gina screamed once, her hands held to her chest, then she whirled and ran into the canebrake that grew tall along the riverbank. Her flight was heavy footed and noisy, canes cracking and twigs snapping to give away her trail.

Lunch picked up the nickel-plated pistol Tiny Baby had dropped, then retrieved his black hat. He set the hat on his head at a Bogartish angle, then began to follow the woman. The golden light cast by the harvest moon imparted a magically real quality to the night. A beautiful light more real than real illumination. As Lunch followed Gina he inhaled deeply, and paused to savor the scene. This river, that moon, this light, those goofy people—yet more evidence of Nature's fantastic production values!

The path Gina had blazed through the canebrake made Lunch's task simple. He slowly followed in her own footsteps until her red dress gave her away. She was trying to hide, all rolled up low to the ground, but the red dress was so brilliant the entire maneuver was a waste of time.

"Hide and seek," Lunch said. "I *see* you!" He stood over her and gave her a soft kick. "Come on, Mary—let's negotiate."

"Don't kill me. Oh, don't."

"You know what? You *look* a lot like my sister, Rayanne, and you *act* like her, too." He grabbed a handful of her blond hair and pulled her up. "Let's check on Tiny Baby."

She walked weakly, her knees all rubbery. Lunch shoved her along, back to the Bug and the headlight beams. When she saw Tiny Baby laying there, bloody and inert, she collapsed beside him.

"I'll do anything you want," she said. She rolled onto her back, the light in her eyes, and looked up at Lunch. "I do great french—anything you want, please, please."

Lunch watched her for a moment, then said, "It's weird—you really *do* look like my sister. She had hair like yours." He squatted beside her, then reached a hand to the top of her red dress and pulled down, baring her breasts. "Whew!"

"Please, please. Anything."

"Too weird!" he said. "So much alike." He put the pistol barrel against her chin and forced her head back. Then he lowered his lips to her left breast and sucked. He circled his tongue around her nipple. "Sweet," he said. "Hers weren't this big."

"Please, pl—"

"No beggin'!" he said. He ran his fingers through her blond hair, tangling his fingers in the long fine locks. "Did Tiny Baby say something?" he asked, and as her eyes swung hopefully toward Tiny Baby he pulled the trigger, and blew her face away in a red pulpy mist. The sound of the blast ran up and down the river, spreading over the water. "So much for forever, sis."

Lunch tossed the pistol into the river, listening to the echo the splash made. He searched Tiny Baby's pockets for cash but found none. Then he found his own cash on the ground, rolled the cash tightly, and tucked it in his pocket. He walked back to the Bug and opened Gina's knitting bag. The thick booklet of money they'd flashed was in there, and he carried it to the headlights to examine. He fanned the bills in the light, and quickly saw that it was a Michigan Roll, five twenties wrapped around two inches of cut paper. All of this for a C-note! What fakers!

His heart sank. He doused the headlights, then stood slouched against the fender of the Bug and smoked Salem number six, exhaling wistful trails of smoke. Another part of the blue leaflet Lunch had read earlier in the day popped into his mind. It dealt with days like this one. The passage was to the effect that the actual river, as well as the river of life, was festooned with innumerable shoals, sucks, snags, and sawyers, all of which posed dangers, both seen and secret, to the craft that floated down them. That was all of the passage Lunch could recall for sure. There may have been a solution or remedy mentioned farther down the page, but he'd just skimmed that part.

When the Salem was burned to the filter, Lunch flipped it into the dark. He opened the bonnet of the Bug where the storage space was on these things. He reached in and grunted loudly as he heaved three large rocks onto the gravel beside Tiny Baby and Gina. "His," he said, then started heaving smaller rocks onto the black graveled earth. "And hers."

# part iii

# Choices

Rene Shade had started his evening off in the community center gym, sitting in the bleachers with his father, watching a bar league basketball game and trying to plumb the depths of his strange love for the power forward in red. Nicole Webb, the high scorer for his affections and on the court, was leading the Peepers, the team from Maggie's Keyhole, against the much feared ladies from Barb'n Bob's Bowl'n Brew. Shade sat impassively next to his father, only occasionally pointing toward the court as the woman in his life flung elbows at ribs, kicked at shins, set vicious moving picks, dove for loose balls, and got into shoving matches with burly, emphatic spinsters as if she wanted this sport and its attendant violence to make a personal choice for her.

"Your lady friend is good to watch," John X. said. "She ain't afraid of contact."

"She doesn't usually play this rough a game," Shade said.

"Well, you're a lucky fella, son. She runs the court very nicely for a pregnant gal."

Out on the hardwood the sweat and curses and jump shots were flying. Nicole's skin had flushed to a temperamental pink, and she'd picked up three fouls and one new enemy in seven minutes of rough play. The expression on her face was as intense and bellicose as it had been earlier, when the subject of the future had come up between Shade and herself. The discussion had been held over cups of coffee at Maggie's Keyhole where Nicole was bartender, and it had been a friendly, open discussion for the first minute and a half. Then Shade had said the routine things about feeling pressured and somewhat roped, and she said a caustic thing about his predictable comments, and from there they went at it in a strained, snapping, he-said-she-said squabble that eventually ended with a to-each-his-own proposition being coolly stated by her, seconded by him.

"I couldn't even guess what marriage to her would be like," John X. said. He lit a Chesterfield and smiled. "The women I've attracted always ran more to the type that are fans instead of players."

Shade said, "Marriage hasn't even been mentioned, Johnny. Lots of other shit has been, though."

The Peepers had a fast break going down-court, and the twenty-five or thirty people in the bleachers made an appreciative murmur as Nicole caught the pass out on the wing and drove toward the hoop, curling around one opponent, then going body-on-body with another as she skyed for the lay-up, and drew the foul. Both women fell to the floor, and when her opponent offered a hand up, Nicole shook her head. She got to her feet and trudged to the foul line, small trickles of blood below both knees.

"She *is* knocked up, ain't she, son?"

"Yeah. Yeah, she is. But don't start stockin' up on cigars just yet."

Watching Nicole from the bleachers, seeing the way she muscled into the paint for rebounds and whipped those hard elbows around, Shade wished he could take back over half the things he'd said to her. The Peepers' jerseys were red with blue lettering, and Nic had on black shorts and bright red sneakers. When she raised her arms to rebound or shoot, lush tufts of dark pit hair were displayed. She moved from hoop to hoop with gangly grace, fluffy pony-tail flopping down her back. Her jump shots were fluid and deadly below the key, and she fought for all of the garbage under the basket.

Probably she *would* make a fine mother, if that was the point.

"Well," John X. said, "I guess you don't have to get hitched these days just because she's pregnant. Plenty of women who are pregnant don't want to either. So they don't. Nobody throws rocks at 'em nowadays."

"What if *I* want to get hitched?"

"You do?" John X. stubbed his smoke out and dropped it between the slats.

"Could be. I don't know."

Down on the court the contest was slipping away from the Peepers. Nicole sat on the bench to take a blow, and the inside game of the large Bowl'n Brew ladies asserted itself. The Peepers began to laugh helplessly on defense, and with the ball they were dispirited and failed to set up any offense other than individual attempts to execute the fabulous. By halftime the Peepers were down by fourteen points. The two teams huddled at opposite ends of the gym. A few voices were raised to shout advice to the desperate. Players from both teams took turns walking slowly to the water fountain.

"I think I'll head for the shed," John X. said, stretching his back. "Not much of a game anyhow." He put his hands in the pockets of his dead man's coat and looked at his son. "But listen, Rene—there always was two things I wanted to never ever do in my life, and I did 'em both. That's right. One was gettin' married, and two was gettin' married *again*. Both times I found myself locked in jail by wrong choices, see. I would've had to draw a picture of Betty Grable on the wall and crawl out the crack to escape."

"What're you saying? You're *legally* married to Etta's mom?"

"Of course I am."

Shade just stared at his dad. "Shit, you mean you've added bigamist to whatever *else* you are?"

"Why, I don't think so, son."

"That's what it is, when you're married to another woman, besides Mom."

"Not besides, son—married *after*ward."

"What are you talking about? That's not what Ma said. You two never got divorced."

"Really? That's what she said?" John X. shakily lit another smoke. "Geez, that's awful romantic of her, son. I can see where she could make it vivid to you boys. I don't mind much. It was one of her talents, you see. But actually, she divorced *me* after I hit the road. Why, the papers finally caught up to me the night I saw you at that fight of yours in Tampa. You must've told her I was comin'."

"I might have," Shade said.

"Criminentlies, remember that fight, son?"

Shade raised his fingers to his broken nose. "That was when I hooked up with that kid they had down there then. Wolburn. Tom-Tom Wolburn. He was quick, but he tired late."

"I remember," John X. said. "He was a will-o-the-wisp type of fighter. He painted your face up pretty gaudy with that jab of his. Pop-pop-pop. He had that mitt on your nose all night long."

"Shit," Shade said. "I busted his guts. He stayed in the hospital for two days pissin' blood. I beat his belly to fuckin' jelly."

John X. shrugged.

"I thought they could've seen it as a draw."

"Draw? I *won* that fight."

"No."

"*I* thought I won it."

"No," John X. said, shaking his head with certainty. "You didn't win it, son, by no means, but they could've called it a draw."

Smoke curled above the two men.

Then, Shade nodded his head, smiled, and said, "His fuckin' jab was a beautiful punch. I couldn't do nothin' with it, and there was no way to hide from it. Bob, weave, peek-a-boo, it didn't matter, the fuckin' jab found me."

John X. inhaled a long slow draw of smoke. As he exhaled he flicked the cigarette down through the bleacher slats. "We saw the same fight, after all, son. Honesty can siphon off a few regrets and resentments if you tap in to it. Let that sink in." He half weaved as he stood, and Shade heard the creaking of his father's knees. "Bleachers are hell on old men." John X. patted Shade's back, then shuffled a few feet down the bleacher aisle. "It's your choice," he said. "See you around, kid."

The second half was more of the same, but Shade kept watching until Nicole fouled out with three minutes to play. The Peepers were down by twenty-three points so he left the gym and began to walk through Frogtown. The sidewalks were dark and uneven. Here and there small piles of leaves had been raked into the gutter and set afire, imparting to the night the smoky, wistful smell of another year gone.

On North Second Street Shade came abreast of the Sacred Heart Academy and took a seat on a bench at a bus stop there. The Sacred Heart encompassed a full city block, and inside the tall iron-pike fence that surrounded it there were beautiful parklike grounds. The night was warm and fallen leaves scuttled in the breeze. Birds roosted in the bare trees, and Shade could see a few sisters strolling past gas lamps that lit the paths inside the fence. Though he'd lived in Frogtown all his life, he'd only been inside the Sacred Heart grounds twice, both times when he was a child, for reasons now forgotten.

For fifteen minutes Shade stared through the pike fence, watching as nuns from the Sacred Heart took their evening stroll, listening to the cadence of their steps and occasional laughter. He resumed his own stroll then, and headed toward Nicole's place on the fringe of the neighborhood.

Frogtown, the oldest quarter of St. Bruno, had been founded by the flocking of outdoorsy miscreants who saw business opportunity in the swamps and the river and the parade of suckers who boated down that treacherous brown flow. It was by now a neighborhood of rowhouses of brick or wood, shotgun apartments, small weary stores, robust vice franchises, and abundant dirt alleys that made for excellent escapes from the scene of the crime. Small backyards were strung with clotheslines from which flapped the work clothes of the occasionally employed, a work force that generally punched the clock on various nearby stools where they drank at the bar, toked in the alley, and gambled upstairs with their cut of the take or this month's disability check, and when that was lost, the last smoke ashes, and the bottles only glass, they posted themselves to the street with their empty pockets held open wide, faces turned to the sky, on a red-eyed alert for that much ballyhooed trickledown of wealth.

Nicole's place was a frail frame house on Perkins Street. Shade went up the steps of the front porch, then took out his key and let himself in. As the door opened into the dark front room, bells tinkled gently against the glass, and he called out a questioning "Nic?" to announce himself. The light from a street lamp fell through the lace curtains on the tall narrow windows of the living room, casting paths of faint blue light across a worn Persian rug. Shade walked through the shotgun apartment, heading toward the back until he saw light seeping out from beneath the bathroom door. He rapped his knuckles gently to the wood. "It's me," he said. He heard water lap against the tub. He pushed on the door and slipped into the small, steamy bathroom that he and Nic had painted a startling shade of peach one Saturday afternoon in the spring. She was lying in the deep water tinted blue from the bath salts she used, her toes curled over the enamel lip of the old clawfoot tub.

"If you half close your eyes," she said, "it's like Cozumel."

"Tough game," he said. Nicole released a long heavy sigh, then, blue water slishing past her breasts, she leaned forward, her hair falling around her face as she stared down into her lap. Shade sat on the edge of the tub, picked up the bar of soap, and began to wash her back with long, unbroken strokes of his hand.

"I been thinking," he said.

When he finished her back and rinsed her with long pours from a plastic beer pitcher lifted from Maggie's Keyhole, Nic pulled the plug chain with her toes, then stood silently, and he handed her a towel. Her knees were scraped, and swollen red from hot water, and he made out the beginning of a long yellow bruise on her upper left thigh. Nic stepped out of the tub, as water cascaded to the tile floor. For a moment she buried her face in the towel, muttered something indecipherable, then padded into the dark bedroom leaving a wet trail of footprints behind. Shade pulled another towel from the rack and kicked it toward the puddle on the bathroom floor. He still kept his own apartment—a tiny bachelor pad in the upstairs of his mother's pool hall—but most nights he curled up against the perfect fit of Nicole's buttocks, in her bed that was, in practice, theirs.

She had dropped herself like a sack of groceries, flat out, face down on the bed. He turned on a night-light on the bed stand. It was a fifties lamp, a plastic cylinder depicting Niagara Falls, with a couple standing beside an overlook above the blue and white waters churning below. "I've been thinking," he said, as he reached for a tube of Ben Gay next to the lamp, then sat down on the bed, and pressed some cream into the palm of his hand.

"Thinking what?" she spoke into the pillow folds.

"About a honeymoon." He rubbed the Ben Gay between his hands. "We could go to Niagara Falls. Something like that." He leaned over her and began to knead her shoulders and her shoulder blades.

"Oh Geez," she said with a groan, but it was unclear to him whether she was saying no or saying yehess to his massaging hands. He worked his hands in circles over her ribs, then down to the small of her back, and she released a long, yielding moan.

When she spoke, however, her voice was monotone. "You want to get married now?"

"I've been giving it some thought," he said.

She tilted her head forward so he could knead the nape of her neck. "Why do you think you want to get married, Rene?"

"It could be the right way to go," he said.

"I'm asking *why*, Rene."

"Well, come on, you know I'm Catholic."

"You're *what*—"

"I'm Catholic. That's what I was baptized."

"Oh, Christ, you're not doing this to me. You're not going to say the Catholic Church is why you have to marry me."

"Okay, okay, forget the Catholic. I don't go anyhow. But maybe I just want to then. I was just sort of spooked before. I was caught off-guard. Here I am on suspension and all—it just seemed at first like *one more thing* that went wrong, and smacked me in the head. I sort of panicked at first, okay? But now I'm getting used to the idea, and if you think about it, I mean, where *are* we going, Nic, if we don't eventually get married and so on." Shade pressed his hands back and forth across her rib cage, then began to knead the muscles in her buttocks.

"I don't know," she said, drawing the words out as he massaged. "You're pretty good at *this*."

Shade moved down to her thighs, and Nicole groaned as her hamstrings stretched with his fingertips. "Thank Chester Anderson for this stuff. Chester taught me everything I know. That old man could draw the pain out through his fingertips. Best rubdown man a fighter like me could ever hope to find."

"Rene," Nicole said through a mouthful of sheets, "you don't even have a job."

"I'll be back with the cops," he said. He slid down on the bed to reach her calves. "This idleness is just temporary."

"You're through with the cops, Rene. You're through. Unless you say you're sorry, or something. Tell them you'll be happy to be their bagman from now on, and knock off anybody they tell you to. Unless you knuckle under you're through as a civil servant." She sighed, and he turned his attentions to her feet.

"Look, Nicole, if I have a family, I *will* provide."

"Oh great—great! I'm not going to be the excuse for you to become evil. I'm just not *fucking* going to be that excuse for you."

"Hold still," he said. "You like the feet part best."

"Rene, Rene, Rene," she said. "What about me? I mean, I never planned to end up in a place like this, a little grubby town where everything gets dirty just hanging in the air. What will I become? I'm a bartender, for chrissake.

I could be something different. I just never planned to sling suds forever."

"You never planned anything," he said. "That's why you're a bartender." He rubbed the ball of her foot, but her foot was taut, resisting him. "So you're a bartender, anyhow, so what?"

"I wanted to go back to Europe, especially to Spain," she said. "Could we go live in Spain? I mean, what do you care about St. Bruno, anyway?"

"Spain?"

"Barcelona. Costa Del Sol. Ibeza. There's a world of blue water out away from here."

"You gonna keep drifting all your life?"

"I like new places. I'm a traveler."

"Yeah, right. You oughta talk to my dad about that. About traveling." He let her foot drop to the bed. He stood over her prone body.

"I love you, Nic. I want to marry you. I'm asking you to marry me. Have the little thing. Crumb snatcher crawling on the floor. Drooling and squalling, I can handle that. Not just one, though. It's bad to have one kid. If you're gonna have one, have—three. Three's a good size."

"*Three?* You're out of your fuckin' mind, man," she said. She sat up and pulled on a robe. "My God, you *are* a Catholic—a frigging Catholic—"

"So what's it going to be? Do you love me, or what?"

"Or what? Or what? I love you," she said, "but I've got to think." She looked at the blue night lamp. Inside there was a fettered wheel above the bulb, and when it heated up enough the slatted wheel turned round and round causing an illusion of white water roiling upward from below the falls. They had picked up the lamp at a flea market for fifteen bucks. It seemed like a lot for celluloid, but they liked the notion of an idealized Niagara Falls forever cascading inside the lamp, so they bought it anyway.

"We're not going to Niagara Falls," she said. "I can tell you that."

"What does that mean?" He took hold of her shoulders and pulled her face closer. "What does that mean?"

"It means I'm not going to act impulsively. We're talking about deep shit here, Rene. The rest of our lives. If we're lucky we'd still be kickin' when our little ingrates would go off to the state university, or the vo-tech, or maybe just down to the corner for a few zillion drinks."

Shade leaned to her until he could smell the faint scent of jasmine and musk in her hair, then he brushed his lips across her forehead just below the hairline. "So you're going to think about it?"

"Yeah. I'm gonna think about it *all*. You bet I am." She patted his rear end the way two athletes do between plays. A dismissal of sorts. "You'd better sleep at your place tonight," she said. "I've got things to sort through."


As Shade came down Lafitte Street, walking through a light mist, he saw that the lights were all on in Ma Blanqui's Pool Room, which meant his mother had customers. When he reached the door he saw his brother Francois's white Volvo parked down the block, the shiny import seeming to gleam amid the domestic heaps.

There was some straight pool education going on at the front table, the lessons being taught by J. J. Guy, who lived in a flop across the street, and absorbed by Henry DeGeere, a neighborhood fella who had, by local standards, gotten rich off the gas business, but who still couldn't run six balls to save his life.

"J. J.," Shade said. "Henry."

Both of the older men nodded and said, "Rene."

There were two teenaged boys at the center table playing eight ball, no slop, call your pocket, and though Shade had seen them all over the neighborhood he knew them only as the Freckle-Faced Kid from around the corner, and the Four-Eyed Chubby Kid who lives where the Pelligrinis used to. They both knew him, though, and Freckle-Face said in a mocking drawl, "What's happenin', off-i-cer?"

Shade stopped, and said, "What you *want* to happen?"

Freckle-Face got interested in his next shot. He kept his face down, scrutinizing the green felt.

"Nothin'," he said.

"That sounds right," Shade said, and walked on toward the back where he could see his mother on her high stool behind a red Dr. Pepper cooler, a wide cooler that his younger brother was now leaning against.

Francois, the tallest of the Shade brothers, was a lean man with carefully styled dark hair, and the sartorial flair of a Latinate dandy. He was an Assistant D.A. and lived in Hawthorne Hills in a landmark home his wife, Charlotte, had inherited. The suit jacket he wore was of a smoked silver color, over a pale blue shirt now open at the collar, a gray striped tie dangling from a jacket pocket.

"It's your birthday, Ma," he said to Monique, "just tell me what you want."

Monique had her long gray hair braided and pinned up like a crown. She wore horn-rimmed glasses that magnified her eyes, a black cigarette dangling from her lips.

She was dressed in khaki trousers, a green army shirt, with pink fuzzies on her feet.

She was looking at Rene's approach as she said, "How's about world peace, and a river of beer?"

Shade leaned against the cooler beside Francois, who said, "We'll save that for Christmas, Ma."

"What's up?" Shade asked.

Francois patted him on the shoulder.

"Trying to get her to confess on the subject of what she *really* wants for her birthday."

Monique turned her magnified eyes on Shade, pointing at him with the black cigarette.

"One thing I want is for you to be good to Nicole, you rat." She jabbed the smoke in his direction. "You hurt that girl, son, and I *will* take a fuckin' skillet to your head."

"I love you, too, Ma," Shade said. "Now butt out."

"What's up with Nicole?" asked Francois.

"Nothin'," Shade said.

"Hah," went Monique, "that's a man talkin' there."

"Oh," said Francois. "I think I get it."

At the front table Henry groaned loudly over some sort of pool injustice, and Shade looked that way.

"Saw the old man tonight," he said. "He doesn't look too good."

"How could he?" Francois said. "He's been holed up in a bottle for thirty years, at least."

"He don't look too good, but he can still be pretty funny," Shade said.

"Don't I know it," Monique said. "His sense of humor got you boys born. Tell me about this daughter he's got now."

"Well," Shade said, "she's a weird kid."

"I always wanted a daughter," Monique said, smoke clouding around her face. "It just wasn't to be."

Shade turned to Francois, and said, "You ought to drop in on the old fart. He's stayin' over at Tip's. This girl, her name is Etta, she's half your sister, Frankie."

"No," Francois said. He spun away, his eyes on the pool players. His clean teeth scraped at his lips. "He's a phantom to me. That's all—a fuckin' phantom. I don't want anything to do with him." He raised his left arm and looked at his watch. "I'm late. I've got to get home." He smacked his hand on top of the cooler. "See you for your birthday party, Ma."

He patted Shade's shoulder once more as he walked toward the door.

When the door closed behind Francois, Monique asked, "So what's this li'l girl of Johnny's like? Is she pretty?"

"That's hard to say, Ma. Her hair is cut funny, and she's been taught to use, like, Crayolas, on her face. She's a sight."

"L'il girls are different, son."

"This one sure is," Shade said. He yawned and stretched his back against the Dr. Pepper cooler. "I'm crashin' upstairs tonight."

Monique regarded him coolly from behind another black cigarette.

"That's interestin'," she said.

"I'll tell you what's interestin', Ma," Shade said. "You know how you always told us you'n Dad were still married, legally? How he was just a runaway husband and daddy, runnin' for all these years? Well, the way he tells it is *you* divorced him *years* ago. Years and years, actually."

"That so?"

"Yeah. Why'd you keep tellin' us you were still married if it wasn't true, huh, Ma?"

From her seat on the high stool Monique leaned forward and planted her elbows on the cooler top. Her eyes looked huge behind her glasses. She raised her chin to a belligerent angle, then blew smoke at her son.

"Why, it should be obvious," she said in a caustic tone. "I wanted to fuck with your head, pure and simple."

# 11.

Mrs. Carter had a number of rules. A tallish woman of considerable age, Mrs. Carter was usually attired in a calico dress and plain black shoes, and though the expression on her pinched face suggested an inner, ineffable sadness, she was diligent in the performance of her duties. When new girls came into her house, she sat them down and ran off a short speech to them that explained her various general rules: "A healthy child is what folks want, and it's what they pay for, too. That means we'll have zero vices here. No drinkin', dopin', cigarette smokin', or godawful eatin' habits. You'll eat vegetables in this house. You'll eat lean meats, all varieties of vegetables, lots of fruit and milk, and you'll have no sex. Don't get outside here and meet up with some boy who is just dreamy to you, and his arms are so very, so very, very warm to you, and his tongue darts quick in your mouth and you plumb blow it out your mind that you are fatter'n a blue ribbon pumpkin because you are *preg*-nant, girls. There's a child in you. So, no carnal relations—hear?"

Mrs. Carter's house was ranch style, basically, everything on one floor to avoid the strain of stairs. Gretel and the four other girls didn't do much around the place but languish on the soft furniture and expand. They nibbled at trays of fruit Mrs. Carter set out and watched television from the early morning agricultural reports right up to the late local news, the end of which signaled bedtime. Three of the girls were from the area, with Gretel and one other being the only out-of-state recruits.

The girls talked quite a bit of worried talk about the birthing of their babies. There were rumors of tremendous pain in the delivery process. The girls talked about it like Marines in a foxhole talk about being taken alive. Gretel was quietest on this subject because she'd seen field-hippie women have babies while lying on Navaho rugs in Delirium's kitchen, and they'd come out of it fine, healthy, sometimes joyous.

Mrs. Carter's house was well known in the neighborhood, and once in a while it would be the site of a disturbance. Ex-boyfriends might drive up drunk, screaming insults, or parents would arrive to lecture one of the girls about their deep disappointments in her, then escalate in their anger. Sometimes after dark young boys on spider bikes mooned around on the sidewalk and front lawn, calling out enticements and lusty claims to this household of girls who clearly would *fuck* if they could be lured into the bushes.

The bedroom Gretel slept in was farthest from the kitchen, which discouraged snacking in the early A.M.

hours, but it had a window facing onto the street, and studying the view soon came to be her hobby. Gretel shared the room with Lori, an older woman of twenty-two who'd lived a life of rancid nothingness down on the south side of town, but because of the positioning of the beds, she had the view to herself.

Three houses were constantly in sight, and if she craned her head to wider angles two more houses and a garage were visible. The men of these houses seemed to lead lives similar to those Gretel had been told about by Zodiac and Delirium. These men went off in the mornings fresh-shaven and in crisp-clothes but came home around supper time all tore down by soulless work of some sort, their clothes sagging, their faces weary. Two of the men nearly always carried six-packs of beer to kill their evenings with. The various wives were about perfectly split between going away to work or staying put at home. So many children ran around the worn lawns that she wasn't sure which houses which ones belonged to.

The way these people lived was so weird. They were under the thumb of society to the extent where they probably thought they had it good. Would Zodiac mock them if he was here? For sure he'd flip his gray ponytail at them and bark. He'd bark and grin and sing a song about their humdrummery as loud as he could and possibly do the Pawnee Dance of Doom on the trunks of their cars. Zodiac spent *his* days doing whatever he wanted, the only thumb he came under was Nature's, a fairly ferocious thumb at times, but one he found agreeable. The crop he tended was an Afghani strain called Razorback Red that he'd grown for years on government land, an ungreedy stand of twenty-five plants budding in the Mark Twain National Forest. Generally Gretel and Delirium handled the chores around the house. Delirium gardened and sewed through the daylight hours, then, as darkness fell, she turned to her poetry, which was all concerned with her childhood back in Tarrytown, New York. The poems, some rhyming, some not, spelled out how this childhood in privileged circumstances had turned her away from the shallow urge to own and destroy, and toward the hidden part of herself that society would kill, the part that was best expressed nude, under bright stars, with a reefer in one hand and the laughter of freedom pealing from her lips.

When darkness fell on this street, the people of all five houses closed in around TV sets. They didn't come out again until their alarm clocks made them.

Weird. But interesting.

Gretel was sitting cross-legged on her bed, letting her skin breathe, watching the street, when Tip slowly drove by in his big ol' gas-eater car. She rolled carefully off the bed and went down the hall to the bathroom. She ran some water and splashed her face. She slipped into a green dress, brushed her hair, then went into the front room. The other girls were all gathered there, ignoring the sitcom on the tube, making jokes about Tom's child.

"Tom's child is kickin' this evenin'," Lori said.

"Tom's child is healthy," said Carol.

"And so damn cute!" said Dorothy.

The four of them giggled, their big ripe bodies wallowing on the soft furniture. This Tom's child business was the house joke, a variety of unwed mother humor. All of the girls had wearied of explaining who they knew or thought or hoped was the father of their baby, and after a few bull sessions Carol had loftily claimed that the man responsible for her condition was none other than Tom Cruise, the cutest dude in the galaxy, and after a moment of silence, Gretel had said, "Well, me, too." Pretty soon it developed that all five women believed themselves to have been knocked up by the very same movie star dick, and from there on all referred to their common burdens as Tom's child.

"I'm takin' Tom's child to a movie," Gretel said. "Show him his daddy, maybe."

"You take good care of my man's child," Carol said.

On her way out Gretel encountered Mrs. Carter on the front porch. Mrs. Carter smoked a pack and a half of Marlboros per day, but, in keeping with her own rules, she only smoked on the outside porch.

"Where you goin'?" she asked.

"A movie."

"Seems like you've been goin' to a lot of movies."

"I enjoy them. I hardly saw any back home."

"Uh-huh. Where do you get the money?"

"The movie money?"

"Uh-huh."

"Today—a man gave it to me."

"Ah." Mrs. Carter stuck her cigarette in the big sand ashtray she kept on the porch. "Why'd he give money to you?"

"I watched his dog."

"His dog?"

Tip's car was not in view.

"While the man shopped. At Krogers. His dog has run away twice this week, and he didn't have a chain with him, so I said I'd watch."

"Uh-huh."

"It was an Irish Setter." She looked down the street. "Named Bono."

Mrs. Carter lit another Marlboro. She flicked the dead match on the lawn.

"You be home early."

Gretel went walking down the sidewalk, occasionally placing her hands under her belly and hefting. One of those dirty little boys trailed her on a spider bike for a minute, wheeling up close to her side and breathing heavy, but on his own like this he didn't have anything foul to say, and soon pedaled away.

Around the corner and halfway down the block Tip was waiting on her. The night was warm, his windows were down, and she could hear his radio tuned in, as always, to a Golden Oldies station, blaring "White Rabbit," a song Delirium had often sung to her when she was young.

When Gretel slid into the car Tip started the engine, grinned at her, and pulled away from the curb.


Pio's Italian Garden was a spot of make-believe Brooklyn, a loving re-creation of the joints Pio had known during his childhood back in the Red Hook section of what he often called "the old country." The authentic touches in this decorative homage were the vast scenes of Neapolitan kitsch that were painted on the walls, the small square tables with red-and-white checkered cloths, the DiNobili cigars in the glass case below the cash register, and the jukebox on which Ol' Blue Eyes was the boss songster, backed up by a goombah choir of underboss songsters mostly named Tony.

One painted wall depicted a spectacular scene wherein a Naples tenement was built at an angle that extended far enough over the bay that a chubby mama with a big toothy grin could fling a platter of linguini from a third floor window across the sailboats and yachts to a wedding group dining al fresco on the Isle of Capri.

Tip leaned back in his chair, pulling away from a plate of savory manicotti he was too nervous to eat. Gretel sat across from him, slowly chewing a meatball, her eyes intent on the wall painting. Despite all the spice in the air, he could smell her, her certain scent. She smelled so sweet, but not of perfume. This fragrance of hers couldn't be bought in a bottle. It was a scent that must rise from the spirit or soul, then waft from her pores, her hair, that huge bulge, or perhaps that scar. He raised his nose and sniffed.

Gretel turned her face from the wall, and said, "I don't believe that's accurate."

"The mural?"

"It's not like that abroad. Zodiac's been everywhere."

In his red shirt with black buttons, black sports coat and slacks, with his glistening brown hair swept back and hanging to his shoulders, big Tip looked potentially dangerous but sincerely spruced. A series of curious smiles kept coming to his pocked face. These smiles were small in stature, but quick and relentless.

"I'd like to take you there," he said. "Rome."

Chewing, Gretel pointed a fork at the wall, then swallowed.

"It won't look like that. Don't get your hopes dashed."

"By boat, maybe," he said. Three quick smiles. "Or do you get seasick?"

"I don't know," she said. She touched four fingers to her scar. "On curvy, hilly roads I *can* get carsick. Maybe the sea is different."

"By plane would probly be best," Tip said.

"I haven't had better food," Gretel said, her fork

wrapping up a wad of spaghetti. "I like these meatballs, even though I realize animals have personalities. Spirits, even."

Tip smiled. "I couldn't see me livin' on vegetables alone."

"Some say cows are sacred. Did you know that, Tip? That cows are sacred?"

"Smothered in Pio's sauce, they're even better'n *that*," Tip said, smiling, laughing, tapping his fingers on the table.

Gretel made a happy face.

"You're funny."

"You're beautiful."

"Come again?"

Tip planted both elbows on the table and leaned forward.

"I haven't kissed you, but you're so *beautiful*, Gretel."

"I feel good inside. I try to have up vibes, and not down vibes."

"No," Tip said. His big hands went to his hair and messed it up. Long slick strands flopped over his face. "What I mean is, I want you to stay after your baby is born."

"That'll be soon," Gretel said. "It's s'posed to be another month—but I don't think so."

"I want you to stay with me."

"Sure." Gretel raised a napkin and wiped her mouth. "I could likely use a place to crash by then—I won't be welcome at Mrs. Carter's no more."

"God," Tip said. He looked around the restaurant, not really seeing anything. "I don't mean to crash—I want you to marry me, Gretel."

Her fork dropped. "That's too far out."

"I can't imagine living without you."

Tip's face showed doubt, and fear, and nervous hope. He was smiling too much and knew it, and rather forcefully asserted control over his features, composing his face to meet possible disaster.

Gretel said, "Marriage is ownership, Tip. Domination. There's a pretty flower in the forest, let's say, and what is marriage but the pluckin' of that flower so's it can be worn in a buttonhole. Like a decoration. A plucked flower in a buttonhole can only wilt, man, and it won't never bloom again."

"I guess I don't follow," Tip said sullenly.

"It's murder by ownership," Gretel said.

The clock was pushing toward ten, and the Italian Garden was fairly quiet. Near the front window from which a red neon pizza beamed onto Fifth Street, a silver-haired gent in a tasteful linen suit split a meatball grinder with a golden-haired boy in street leather. The organizers of a just-ended Knights of Columbus fund-raiser were relaxing at a big table in the center of the room, and Monsignor Escalera was pouring the beer. At the back of the room, in their regular booth next to the pay phone, a couple of Frogtown boys loitered over plates of mussels and glasses of rosé, studying tomorrow's nags in the Racing Form.

"I make decent money," Tip said. He picked up his fork and rolled the manicotti on his plate. "I've got a comfy set of wheels." He forced his fork down on the pasta tubes and chopped them. "My house ain't much, but I own it *outright*."

One of the K of C crowd dropped some quarters in the juke and punched in Ol' Blue Eyes. The first song was

"Summer Wind," and the wistful lyrics got to Tip. With nervous fingers he wrecked his hairdo altogther, then sighed.

"I'm sorry you feel this way," he said.

"Tip, marriage and all that—it ain't the way I was raised."

"You'd be taken care of good."

"Freedom is what we value. It comes from *within*. Society, and rules, and all that is what takes it away." Gretel leaned forward. Her face had an earnest expression. "I can't get into marriage, Tip, but I've been wantin' to live with you. I've had it in mind for a while now."

Tip's pocked face raised. He looked into her eyes.

"You have?"

"Uh-huh."

"Well that'd be alright," he said eagerly. "Give it a try, anyhow."

"I do dig you," Gretel said. "We've never got naked together, but I've thought about it some, and I think we'd fit."

"When *I* think about it we sure do," Tip said. He stretched his huge arms and sighed with relief. His face relaxed. "And I've thought about it plenty, though we ain't even kissed before."

"We will," Gretel said. One of the many Tonys was now singing "Jeepers Creepers," raising the spirits all around. "But there's a few things I want in my future. In the place I live, I mean."

"Name them, Gretel. I want what you want."

She took a sip of her soda, and lowered her eyes.

"This is embarrassing," she said, "but at home we don't have flush toilets. Delirium always says the simpler life is the better, but I think I'll have flush toilets from now on."

"Well, hell—I've got *flush* toilets."

"You do? That's primo to me. I've got used to 'em at Mrs. Carter's."

Tip waved his hand in the air and leaned back in his chair.

"Electric lights, gas stove. I've got all that. My fridge ain't too good, though."

"Air-conditioning?"

"Huh?"

"I like air-conditioning, though I know it just enriches the greed heads."

"A window job," Tip said. "It does pretty good. I could get another one."

"I'll buy it," Gretel said. She patted her belly. "I should clear right at fifty-two hundred dollars the lawyer says."

Tip shook his head, long slick hairs flying.

"That's none of my business," he said.

"I won't be afraid to spend it, neither."

Her hands were on the table, and Tip reached his own across and grabbed them. He held tight.

"This is great," he said.

After a few more minutes of silent happiness, Tip and Gretel left Pio's, Tip leaving a ten-dollar bill for their waitress. They walked together out to the parking lot. A light mist was falling and the moonlight was diffused by the clouds. They held hands, ignoring the fine drops, shuffling slowly to his car.

"What about showin' me that house," Gretel said. "You've never took me there before."

Tip pulled his keys out and jangled them.

"Comin' right up," he said. Then he threw his arms around her, pulling her to him sideways to avoid her belly. She turned her face up to his and they kissed, standing in the rain. The first kiss was so swell it immediately led to another. Tongue met tongue, and Gretel put a hand on his ass, then slid it around, squeezing. "Oooh, Gretel," he said, "let's go."

He started to open the car door, but she said, "Wait." She raised her left hand, spread her fingers, and crooked her pinkie. "Tip, give me your finger." He raised his hand, and they entwined pinkies.

Gretel squeezed and said, "That means as much to me as any piece of paper."

# 12.

The house was dark, though no one was asleep. Etta lay on her cot in the kitchen, Tip's transistor radio near her ear, tuned to a rock station, listening to George Michael sing "I Want Your Sex," while John X. lay on the couch in the front room, *his* radio playing "Apple Blossom Time" by the Andrews Sisters.

To keep his mind off of the many possible or certain disasters in his future, John X. was fantasizing, conjuring up an earlier version of himself poised over a regulation Brunswick table, running racks of balls, sinking table-length cut shots, three-ball combos, sophisticated bank shots, constantly drawing the bright white cue ball into perfect shape for the next stroke. This remembered self was having a great time back there in the past, dazzling a crowd of faceless sports and dames, these memories thick with smoke and musk and derring-do. Glorious runs of sixty to ninety balls were routine but fully imagined.

In the midst of a fantastic run, with his former self drawing the Balabushka back from the cue ball, the tip raised to apply top, one of the faceless sports in the crowd stepped forward, into John X.'s line of sight, and suddenly had a face.

John X. jerked up on the couch. His ribs ached from Stew's punches, and now his gut ached with anxiety.

"Criminentlies," he said. "Lunch."

He reached to the side table and turned on a lamp. He could see the kid in the kitchen, curled on the cot, her back to him. He lit a Chesterfield, then walked across the room to the telephone. He sat on a straight-backed chair and dialed information, got the number he needed, then punched it in.

After four rings his call was answered.

"Chapman residence. Mr. Chapman speaking."

"Rodney? It's me—John X. Can you talk?"

"Okay. Yes." Rodney's voice was strained, uncomfortable. "I don't know where you might be, John, and *please, please* don't tell me, but you better be hidden well."

"He's after me, is he?"

"Yes. He was here. He basically *raped* Dolly, looking for you."

"Aw, shit, Rodney—I'm sorry. That's terrible."

"We've begun to see a counselor. The whole thing was awful. It wasn't really your fault, John, but I can't help blaming you."

"I'm sorry, believe me." John X. sucked on his cigarette. "I guess he was brutal, huh? Did you tell him anything?"

"He might've killed us, John. It wouldn't have bothered him to do it, not at all."

"Oh, I know that. Lunch is a killer. But did you tell him anything?"

There was a pause, a telling silence.

"I don't know where you are, John, and I don't want to, but if you and Randi and that girl of yours should happen to be in a town called St. Bruno, well, I think I'd be moving along very promptly."

"Shit!" John X. shouted. He slapped the phone down, slamming the receiver into the cradle. He bowed his head, groaned, and rubbed his temples.

When he raised his eyes, Etta stood before him. She wore boxer shorts and a white tank top, her right hand twirling the black crucifix that hung from her ear.

She said, "What now?"

"Aw, kid—Jesus—do you know what fate is?"

"Uh-huh."

"You *do*?"

"Yeah," she said. "Like if your mom is chubby and crosseyed, probly you'll be chubby and crosseyed, too."

"That's something else," John X. said. "Fate, see, is a black fuckin' cloud that's always pissin' and moanin' *exactly* over your head. You can't shake it and it won't butt out. That's what fate is, kid, a Nosey Parker that meddles with you from the cradle to the grave."

The kid backed to the couch and slumped down.

"You know something about that guy Lunch," she said. "Don't you, Dad?"

He raised his eyes, looked at her, and nodded.

"You're a smart kid, Etta. I must've been sober when I made you."

"Huh. Not likely."

"Watch your lip, angel, I got quite a bit of Sluggo in me tonight." John X. stood and began to pace. "Tonight, you don't want to goad me." He took a few steps toward the door, stopped, clenched his fists and shook them overhead, then turned to his daughter. "We gotta run again, kid."

"Oh, Dad, no!"

"Yeah, kid. I hear the call of the open road again."

"I *like* it here!"

"We better heed the call, kid."

"But Dad," Etta said stridently, "there's family here! We've got family here!"

The old man lit another weed, then sat beside the girl. His hands weren't too steady, and his aching ribs required him to sit hunched forward. His breaths all finished in muted sighs.

"Now kid," he said, "for people like us *the family* is only just a resting place between adventures. You'll need to adjust yourself to that. That's how it is. That's the way us types live."

"But, Dad," Etta said, "Tip is tough. Rene is tough, too, so why do we got to run from Lunch?"

"Aw, kid—Lunch is a ferocious fella. He's a gun-man."

"Dad, that guy's only about this much taller'n *me*. You already knocked him out once, all by yourself."

"I got lucky."

"Now you got Tip and Rene to help."

"My trouble ain't their trouble."

"They'll help."

John X. searched for the ashtray, then stubbed the Chesterfield out.

"We're gonna be broke soon, anyhow," he said. "This poker game ain't gonna bring in the bacon I'd hoped for."

"Uh-huh."

"We can't get by on it."

"I hear you, Dad."

Both radios had continued to play, and John X. and Etta sat together on the couch, sagging, sighing as two very different kinds of music fugued badly, grating on the nerves, Dick Haymes singing "Little White Lies," while Van Halen threw "Jump" into the musical mix.

John X. said, "I need to think—go turn that crap off."

"It's not crap."

"Turn it off anyway."

Etta sat there, hugging her knees, twisting the black crucifix absently, staring at the floor.

"Turn it off, kid—it's janglin' my thoughts."

"Okay, okay," she said, then lurched forward and walked across the room, slapping her bare feet to the floor. She turned the radio off, then got on all fours and pulled the Joan Jett suitcase from underneath the cot. She flipped the lid, carefully ran her hands past Grampa Enoch's bass lures, past her few clothes, to the money hidden in the bottom of the box. She looked at John X. on the couch, then quickly grabbed a handful of cash.

"Dad," she said as she returned to the front room, "I didn't tell you a lie."

"Did I say you did? About what?"

The kid leaned against the wall, poised on one leg, rhythmically swinging the other foot lightly over the floor.

"What I mean is, you never asked, so I never lied."

"That covers an awful lot of ground," John X. said. "Questions I never asked you."

She slowly walked toward him, hands behind her

back, her pale girl legs seeming preposterously long beneath the white boxer shorts. When she reached him she brought her hands from behind her back.

"This is from Mom," she said. "It's my college money. You have to pay after the twelfth grade."

John X. snatched the money from her hand. He reared back on the couch, his eyes narrowed.

"A conspiracy, huh?" he said. "You and Randi cooked up a deal. A deal that cut *me* out."

"I just now cut you in, Dad," Etta said.

She stood there, waiting for some sort of punishment, not knowing what form this punishment might take, or even what was possible, since he'd never spanked or smacked or yelled at her much. "You never asked."

The night was warm, quiet, the eternal murmur of the big river and the radio announcer's voice were the only sounds. The voice was going on and on about world events, reciting the latest news at the top of the hour.

"This hurts," John X. said as he counted the money. "Kid, it really hurts—do you like her more than me?" His fingers snapped each bill onto the cushion beside him with a flourish, the flourishes becoming broader as the count went higher. "Don't answer if you don't want to."

"No," she said.

"Ah, ha—there's nine hundred and fifty bucks here, darlin'!" He began to laugh. He slapped his thigh. "This calls for a drink, angel—where's my bot—"

Steps creaked on the porch, and John X. anxiously looked toward the door. He placed a finger to his lips, motioning for silence. A footstep sounded, and as it did he raised a cushion from the couch, dropped the money in, and brought Enoch's Bulldog .38 out.

"Get in Tip's room," he whispered. "Hide. Don't come

out no matter what you hear." His blue eyes were wide. "You've been a great kid." His daughter hadn't moved yet, and in a harsher voice he said, "Now!"

Then she was gone in a light rush of pattering feet. John X. cocked the pistol, his hand wavering, and slid to the dark screen door. When the steps came closer he aimed, then said in a low, confident voice, "Do you believe in miracles?" He shoved the screen door open, the pistol raised for a point-blank shot. " 'Cause it'd be a fuckin' miracle if I missed you from here."

The figure on the porch was dressed in white, carrying a shotgun. Stew Lassein said, "I don't know why I brought this." He held the shotgun with one hand on the barrel. "I s'pose I've been considerin' killin' you, Johnny."

"You ain't got a chance, Stew. Set that duck gun down right there. Drop it."

The shotgun clattered to the deck. Stew calmly looked at the pistol barrel trained on his face, smiling as if it were an ice cream cone or a strange carnation. John X. backed into the house, the .38 held high, and Stew followed him into the dimly lit front room.

"Criminentlies, but did you give me a start, buddy. I thought you might be somebody else." The light cast by the one lamp illuminated a ruined Stew Lassein. His attire of apparitional white was now soiled, and blood had dried into dark streaks on the shirtfront. He was very pale, and black circles had formed under his eyes. His upper lip was swollen to thumb size. A strong fetid smell wafted from his clothes and body. "Oh, man," John X. said, "have a seat. You look like shit warmed over, buddy."

Stew fell to the couch in sections, like a cargo carelessly unpacked, and sprawled across the cushions.

"Go on and shoot me, Johnny," he said. His chin

touched his chest. "My life was finished last winter, the day that ice storm hit."

"I don't want to shoot you. That's a sad fuckin' state-ment for a man to make, anyhow, ain't it? 'Shoot me,' I mean."

"I just don't care. I ain't been to sleep since the night before last. Since the poker game."

"Well, no wonder."

"I can't. I can't sleep."

John X. took a seat beside Stew on the couch. The pistol sagged in his hand.

"I know you hate me," John X. said, "but I don't know why."

"You know why."

"Sure, there's water under the bridge, but we ain't in it, face down. That's the main thing, right?"

Stew snorted. "That's nowhere *near* bein' the main thing."

"I see. I'm full of shit?"

"Just shallow. So damned shallow. Life is about nothin' but creature comforts to you, and the many like you."

"That's shallow?"

"It's damned shallow."

"Are fuckin' and drinkin' and gamblin' creature com-forts?"

"Oh, yes. Yes."

"Then you're right—I'm one shallow S.O.B."

For a moment Stew was quiet, his eyes open but his mind lost in potent remembrance. A Glenn Miller medley sounded from the radio. When he came out of the past and turned to John X., he made eye contact for the first time since sitting down.

"So, tell me," Stew said, "was Della a good piece of ass?" John X. merely looked at him, unmoving. "I mean it—was Della a good roll in the hay, by your standards?"

"Aw, please, shut up. Don't speak that way about the dead."

"She was my wife, and I thought she was so pretty."

"She was, Stew. A gorgeous kid."

"I never had your gift with the gals, Johnny. I never bowled 'em over the way you did. In high school I screwed a few yaller gals over at Reena Lovett's place, the one she had in that big ol' house by the park."

"A splendid whore house," John X. said. "Reasonable prices."

"And one night I walked home from Uncle Dot's Café with this girl from around here—Olive Thiebault—did you know her?"

"I don't think so."

"She invited me in, and we sat in the kitchen for a while, then we smooched for a while, then she told me it was that time of the month and she couldn't screw, so right there at the table, with her daddy snorin' in the next room, she pulled my thing out and sucked it. I groaned so loud I expected to be murdered before I could get out of there."

John X. laughed, then lit a cigarette.

"How about a drink?" he asked.

"Maybe a week after that I asked Della to go dancin' with me." Stew sighed. "And that's it. That's all the women I ever knew that way."

"Really? Criminentlies—you're gonna make me cry, Stew."

"So you see, I can't make comparisons the way you can. Huh-uh. That's why I have to ask this to know for sure—was my wife a good fuck?"

"Aw, Stew."

"If you said she was, compared to the many, many gals you've humped, Johnny, why, I think it'd cheer me up. I could say, Hey, Stew, you spent most of your life rollin' in the arms of a special piece of tail." Stew slowly stood up from the couch. His weak legs sagged. "That'd be good to know, uplifting." He loomed over John X., his white arms fluttering up and crossing over his chest. "Just the thought of you ruined my marriage. You put a shadow over every kiss I ever got from my own wife."

John X. couldn't raise his eyes. He nervously tapped his cigarette and squirmed on the couch.

"So, Johnny, please, tell me—was Della a special bit of poontang?" His voice raised, cracking. "Was she a nice hump? Good piece of tail?"

"Aw, shut the fuck up!"

"Or just a little on the side, somethin' to pass an hour with while her husband busted his ass at work?"

Stew uncrossed his white arms, placed his hands on John X.'s shoulders, then began to slide them toward his neck.

John X. sat perfectly still, his pistol hanging down, limply, between his knees. He softly said, "Keep it up, and I'll *give* you an answer, buddy."

"Please, tell me."

The hands of Stew Lassein began to slowly close.

"She was really put together," John X. said. "You know that. Nice figure."

"Yes?"

"She smelled good, great kisser, and if you rubbed her titties she'd . . ."

"Oh! Oh!"

Stew fell over backward, his body thumping hard to

the floor, not getting even a hand down to break his fall. He sprawled on his back, lips sputtering, eyes closed, his fingers digging frantically at his chest, breath wheezing. Then, with foreboding swiftness, he was still, and a long, long, long breath of air rushed from his body, whistling an acute, sad song past his false teeth.

John X. stayed on the couch, not bothering to look at Stew. He sat in stunned silence, smoking, then lit another cigarette from the butt of the last, and smoked it down. He dropped this butt into the ashtray, then slid off the couch, and bent over Stew. He looked down at the dead man's face and nodded.

He squatted on the floor, touched the back of his hand to Stew's cheek, and said, "You wanted to know."

When the voices in the front room had quieted, and stayed quiet for what seemed like a long time, Etta cracked the door open and peered out. She could see her dad's head above the couch back, tilted down and unmoving. There'd been some hot voices audible through the door, and one loud thump, so she didn't know what on earth might have happened. She slowly began to move toward her dad, in the lamplight, stealthily stepping in bare feet, her fingers pinched to her boxer shorts and pulling out the slack to avoid telltale rustling.

The man in white, the man who'd cried during poker and claimed to have a scarred heart at the bar, was on his back. Not breathing. And there was Dad, squatting beside the corpse, squatting still as a stone.

Etta came closer and looked at the dead man's face. His mouth was yawned wide, his eyes were narrowly open.

"Oh, Dad," she said, her voice sounding strangely mature and disappointed. "You killed him."

John X. did not raise his head, but he shook it.

Quick confident footsteps came up the stairs, across the deck, and to the door.

Tip's voice sounded, saying, "It's not a bad place, Gretel. The river floods, but there's a good feeling here. I call it home. I like it. Mainly, I guess, because it's paid for."

The screendoor jerked open. Tip and Gretel came in and immediately stopped.

"No, not here!" Tip said. "You had to kill him in *my* house?"

John X. looked up.

"I didn't kill him," he said.

The Bulldog .38 was in plain view.

"You shot him, didn't you?"

"He had a shotgun, son, but I didn't shoot him. It's out there in the dark."

Gretel looked suddenly weak and weary. "I've got to sit down," she said. She sat on the couch.

Tip knelt beside the body, then rolled the corpse over twice, searching for blood.

"He ain't shot. You didn't shoot him."

"I told you that," John X. said. "Heart attack."

"Mrs. Carter is gonna take a switch to me."

Etta took a seat on the couch beside Gretel.

"I can't stand this," she said.

"Dad," Tip said, "we've got to get him out of here. You and him were known enemies after that fight today. There could be a stink if we call the law."

"I hadn't thought of that."

"We could take him into the swamp . . ."

"No! No way." John X. shook his head, then raised his hands and rubbed his eyes. "Let's just take him home— do you know where he lived, son?"

Tip lugged Stew out to the orange truck in a fireman's carry.

"Whew!" he said. "This guy smells."

John X. trailed his son.

"It's been rough times for him, lately," he said. "But they got worse."

Tip laid the body in the bed of the truck. A light rain was falling, and the night wind was whistling off the river in a creepy falsetto.

John X. got behind the wheel, Gretel slid into the middle, Tip took the window with Etta on his lap. Enoch's truck was slow to start, but finally the engine rolled over and the pistons began to make bickering noises.

"Dad," Etta asked, "what is it you want me to do again?"

"Just knock on her door and tell her who you are. Tell her I'm drunk or something and you need a place to sleep."

"She'll let you in," Tip said. "Ma's okay."

The orange truck rolled through the rainy streets of Frogtown to the corner of Lafitte and Perry. John X. pulled to the curb and Etta hopped out, Joan Jett suitcase in her hand.

"I'll be down to get you tomorrow," John X. said. "Be good."

"Tomorrow's Ma's birthday," Tip said.

"That's strange," John X. said, then drove on, following Tip's directions to Stew's place.

The Lassein house was all lit up. When Tip lifted Stew from the truck bed he was sopping, inert and heavy with rain. He quickly carried him to the porch.

John X. tried the door.

"It's locked," he said.

"Try his pockets," Gretel said.

With Tip holding Stew upright, John X. rummaged through the dead man's pockets. He found the key in the front pocket of Stew's wet white pants, and opened the door. A large stuffed chair was in the corner of the front room, surrounded by newspapers, a pair of slippers on the floor beside it.

"That looks like it could be his favorite chair," John X. said. "Let's put him in it. That way whoever finds him'll think he died kind of happier than he really did."

"Whatever," Tip said.

He hoisted Stew into the chair with the body slumped sideways. The corpse looked freshly showered, cleansed, white hairs boyishly slicked down its forehead.

"Try to set him up with dignity," Gretel said. She grabbed Stew's shirtfront and pulled the body upright. "We've got our own Karma to consider here."

Tip said, "He was just talkin' to you, then crashed over dead, huh?"

"That's right."

"What'd you say to him?"

John X. lit a cigarette and looked around the house. Could I have lived like this? Could I? Would it have been better, richer, in any way finer to be a solid citizen like this? Was it for him? Criminentlies.

"History," John X. said. "My history, mainly, a lot of which is lies."

"I don't follow."

"Oh, son, see, a fella gets out in the world and things will happen, and naturally you *will* react, and pretty soon another thing happens and you react again, and after that you got a history you are known by. A bunch of shit concernin' your reactions to things that happen that follows you around by word of mouth. People who don't really know you know what they think is your history, and in my case that ain't so good."

Gretel had Stew's palms turned up to study them. She said, "Yellow nails—that's no good. Plus, his heart line is crossing his head line with a deeper rut. That won't get it for a happy life."

"Uh-huh," Tip said. Then he turned to John X. His brown eyes were bright. "What was it—did you have a thing with his wife?"

John X., the cigarette slanting from his mouth, took a long look at Stew. He could remember when he'd first married Monique, and as darkness fell he had to call her in from the street out front where she'd be playing with other fourteen-year-olds, smacking a tether ball, or dealing old maid, or shaking up soda bottles and squirting root beer into the air. He would stand on the concrete stoop and call for his young pregnant wife, calling her to come in from play and fix her husband supper, and so often Monique would call back, Come-ing, then show up with one or two of her little friends, saying they would help her cook this special dish or that, some dish he would enjoy, and more often than any other her apprentice wife would be Della, Della Rondeau, the cute, cute dark kid who'd lived in these rooms for forty years, with a man who loved and feared her.

"Oh, I've got to go," John X. said. He walked to the door, pausing to cast one last look at Stew Lassein. His benediction was simple: "Que sera and so on, slick."

# 13.

Lunch Pumphrey put his tiny black boots on the window-sill and sat back with his hands behind his head, trying to put an exact number to the deaths he'd administered. The room was on the fourth floor of The Hotel Sleep-Tite, and from the window Lunch gazed out into the black night and wet streets of St. Bruno. A surly wind had kicked up, and rain howled against the window, spattering violently, the raw weather perfectly attuned to Lunch's mood.

Number One had been the tavern owner in Marietta whose last words were "Wake up, Mac—closin' time." Number Two was the auxilliary cop who'd caught him coming out of an electronics store window at two A.M., and Number Three was the woman who'd gone to the twenty-four-hour laundromat in the cool of the night and accidentally seen him blow the head off Number Two. She'd been

holding a wide wicker basket of clean clothes, standing on
the sidewalk, and when he approached she'd begged, which
he hated, he hated begging, fear was in order, sure, even
resistance, but begging merely made a victim's last moments shameful, which is not the emotion you should want
on your face when you are returned to Nature.

After Number Fourteen, an Italian fella in Daytona
who'd been a thorn in the side of Angelo Travelina, Lunch
lost interest in the arithmetic of murder. What was the point
in adding them up when there would surely be more, possibly many, many more deaths to be harvested by him? At
least one more of them, soon, too. Ol' Paw-Paw. He was
here, Lunch could feel it, hear the old man's death song
hummin' in his veins. And most likely Randi Tripp, the
'Bama Butterfly, would be a bonus crop, and whew! but
would he have that thrush warblin' a few new tunes! And
if that gaudy li'l girl was standing there, lookin' like some
sort of freak dwarf from the future, well, just call her des-
sert!

Lunch stood and stretched, looking around the hotel
room. The room was decorated in Flophouse Classic, with
lamps screwed to tables, tables bolted to the floor, and
faded paintings of one clown in several poses nailed to the
walls. This clown had a red nose, a tattered top hat, and
grimed cheeks and clothes in each of the paintings, but in
one he had a neckerchief bundle on a stick over his shoulder, in another he held a hand of cards, all jokers, and in
another he drank an unknown beverage from a rusty tin
can, the serrated lid still attached to serve as a handle.

Lunch shook his head at the squalor of the joint and
decided that whisky and cocaine were in order. This place
too closely resembled home, home with Granny and Aunt

Edna, and anyplace that reminded him of home made him desperate to get high.

He patted a small bottle from his pocket, opened it, and pinched out a snort of blow for each nostril. He hoovered the powder and began to pace. He never should've let thoughts of home into his mind, for any jail he'd ever been in was kinder to him than home, more affectionate even—except for Rayanne. Rayanne—now he needed whisky to wash that name from his mind.

Lunch picked up the door key and his hat and left the room. The Hotel Sleep-Tite had a lounge on the first floor, and he'd fetch a bottle from there. He took the stairs down four flights, crossed the cruddy carpet of the lobby, and went into the lounge. There was a narrow bar and a bunch of tables with plastic chairs, and the lights were low and blue. The bartender looked about the age of a schoolboy, with curly blond hair, and his T-shirt sleeves were short so his muscles were on view.

"Give me a bottle of Johnny Walker Red," Lunch said.

"We don't have it," the bartender said. "Wrong neighborhood. Plus, I'm not supposed to sell by the bottle."

"State law?" Lunch asked.

"Profit motive, I think."

"Ah." Lunch pulled out a twenty and laid it on the bar. "Give me a bottle of what you got."

"Ten more."

"Ouch!" Lunch said. "But okay."

He forked over another sawbuck.

The bartender set a bottle of House of Usher Scotch in front of Lunch. He leaned forward, and said, "You need a broad to go with that, amigo?"

"How much?"

"Fifty for normal stuff."

"Room four ten," Lunch said. "I'll pay the money to *her*. And tell her to bring a magazine."

"A magazine? What kind of magazine?"

"Any kind, it don't matter. But tell her to bring one."

"Twenty minutes," the bartender said.

Lunch went back to his room.

Back in his room, as the rain battered down, Lunch went deep into the blow and Scotch, constantly pacing, drinking straight from the bottle, getting higher and higher until he felt like he was six feet overhead, hovering aloft with no wings, looking at himself from above.

"Rayanne," he said.

Candlelight would be more appropriate, and histori- cally accurate, but he didn't have a candle so he tossed a Sleep-Tite towel over the lamp to soften the light. If he had a radio, he'd tune it to a shit-kicker gospel station, like the one back home, and listen to nasally delivered musical ser- mons on the topics of eternal love and eternal damnation, while banjos strummed and fiddles whined as an accom- paniment.

Whew, but would that make his whole scene perco- late!

When his door was knocked on, Lunch opened it. A black gal stood there, maybe nineteen, but she could pass for less. She wore white knee boots that glistened, and a snug red miniskirt. Her face was lean, and her eyes were big round browns, which was all fine, but what made her seem like a sign from the other side was her hair, which was cornfield blond and not long, but plentiful.

"Oh, man," she said, "is that a birthmark on your face?"

"Bruise. Car wreck."

"Well, hi, then," she said. "I'm Lushus."

"That's nice," Lunch said. He staggered a little, waving the bottle. "But could you answer to Rayanne tonight?"

"Rayanne? Let's see your money first."

Lunch pulled a roll of green from his pocket.

"I got plenty," he said. "Now what's your name?"

Lushus came inside, then kicked the door shut with a white boot.

"Sugar—it's me, Rayanne."

"You got the Sears Catalog?"

"No, I ain't got no catalog."

"I said for you to bring a magazine."

"Oh." Lushus unslung her shoulder bag and reached inside. She pulled out a copy of *Vogue*. "I got this, sugar."

"Well, now," Lunch said giddily, "that's the new Sears Catalog, Rayanne."

"Just tell me what you want," she said. "I think you have a certain story you want to think you're in. That's fine with me. Just tell me what you want."

"Take a shower," he said. "Leave your hair damp, but come out smellin' of soap."

"This is gonna cost."

"I can pay. Here's a C-note."

Lushus snatched the money.

"Just tell me the story," she said as she began to undress, "and I'll be in it."

"You'll be in it," Lunch said. "Don't worry about that."

Lunch looked away as Lushus stripped. When she went into the bathroom and turned on the shower, he sat on the bed. He pulled out the bottle of powder and snorted. He could hear the whore sudsing away in the shower. He bent over and unzipped his boots and slid them off. Then the shirt, then his trousers. Socks and bikini briefs stayed on. He lay across the bed, belly down, his face over the edge, the magazine on the floor before his eyes.

When Lushus came out of the shower, she asked, "What's next?"

"We're in a farmhouse," Lunch said. "Way back off the hard road, down a rutted lane. Total boonies. Granny can't pay the electric bill, so all we got is this candle. Now come here and cuddle on my back. *I* always turn the pages in the catalog."

Lushus slid onto the bed.

"Lordy, but you sure got plenty of pictures on your body!"

"Not at this age I don't." Lunch opened the magazine. "Looky here, Rayanne—new clothes!"

Lushus spread herself over his body, skin on skin. She smelled of soap and her bones dug into his back.

"So pretty," she said, not even looking at the pages. "I want one of those."

"Rub through my hair, Rayanne. Pick through for lice."

"Lice?"

"I don't have lice at this age—I did then. Do it."

The whore began to pluck her fingers through the killer's hair.

"There's one," she said, and pinched his scalp.

"They made fun of me at school today."

"Who did?"

"The Cranston brothers."

"Oh, those boys are mean."

"And Abel Young."

"Him too? Why they make fun of you for?"

"You know why, Rayanne. My shoes and stuff."

"Now that's awful."

"They said I wore stinky clothes and had head lice."

Her fingers pinched his scalp again and again. "I'm killin' them lice, sugar."

"Looky here—cowboy boots."

"I'll get you cowboy boots—see if I don't."

"You always say that."

"I will, sugar. I want things, too. Nobody ever says a nice thing to me neither."

"I know."

"I'm pretty, ain't I? I'm a pretty girl."

"Uh-huh."

The whore lay her face to the killer's neck, her hands at his shoulders.

"But I can't sing good enough for the choir, so they won't have me in it."

"Someday I'll kill them for you."

"I know you will, sugar."

Lunch reached a hand back and began to slide it over the cheeks of her ass.

"Can we?" he asked. "Granny's asleep and Aunt Edna won't hear us in this room."

"I mean, listen here, I have feelings, *too*."

"Blow the candle out."

Lushus reached across and flicked the lamp off. In the dark, Lunch pushed up from beneath and rolled her over.

He spread her legs, then lowered his lips to her left breast and began to suck. His lips sucked gently at her nipple, his lips moving softly, his little hands cupping both breasts.

"Let me slide you in, sugar."

"Nuh," he said. "We don't do that. We just lay like this together."

He continued to suckle at the whore's breast while rain rattled the window, and her hands came up slowly in the blackness, clasped behind his head, and held on.

"We'll always be together," she said. "Always and always."

Lunch greedily sucked and sucked, until it began to sound as if he were crying. Suddenly he pulled his mouth from the whore's breast.

"Please, Rayanne, don't never turn state's evidence on me. Please, sis, don't never do that."

"Never," Lushus said. "You're too dear to me. You and me are all we have."

He dropped his head onto her chest. His breath was warm on her skin.

"I'd have to kill you if you did that."

His lips found a nipple in the dark, and Lushus once again held his head in her hands.

"Oh, sugar, this story is gettin' too sad."


The rains had ended during the night, and as a gray, pearly dawn arrived Lunch came awake, his senses sharp, and saw Lushus standing at the bureau, stealing his roll of green.

Her white knee boots shined, and her red dress fit

her like a sheath. Her golden hair hung to her shoulders. She had the entire roll in her fist, preparing to take it all.

"Lookin' for a match?" Lunch asked. He spun off the bed, shook loose Salem number one, and lit it with a butane lighter. "I can give you a light."

"I'm not *stealin'* this, li'l brother," Lushus said. She kept her back turned to him. "I thought I'd pay Granny's 'lectric bill, sugar."

"How nice of you."

"Then," she said, turning to look him in the face. "I was fixin' to fetch breakfast for my *favorite* brother."

Lunch nodded. All he wore was his black bikini briefs, his many tattoos on clear display, and as he advanced on the whore it was like a small private collection of bad art swaggering forward.

"Brother?" he said as he reached her side. "I look like a nigger to you?" He sidled close to her, then punched her in the belly. "If you were kin to me, I'd be a nigger."

Lushus took the punch pretty well, then raised her fists and swung back at him. Lunch smiled, and punched her again. She sagged, and the money tumbled from her hand, fluttering to the carpet.

"You're all the same," he said. He grabbed hold of her blond hair, flicked his lighter, and held the flame to her thick locks. The hair ignited, and blue fire spread up the strands, crinkling, smoking, stinking.

"Evil!" Lushus shouted. Her hands rose to her blond hair, but the fire was too hot. She closed her eyes and ran to the bathroom, smoke and stink hanging in the air. She jumped into the white tub and put her head under the faucet, kneeling, and turned the water on. As the water doused the flaming hair, soaking her, the whore murmured and hissed.

Lunch stood in the doorway, calmly smoking, watching as the whore's hair became a strange new, two-tone color: blond and burned.

"I ain't got no sister," he said.

# 14.

On Sunday mornings when the spirit was in her, a quest-ing, vengeful spirit, Monique Blanqui Shade slipped into grungy clothes, heavy boots, and a frayed straw hat, and tromped down the tracks toward the Marais Du Croche swamp to slay a few serpents. There were rituals to the hunt. First she'd set the heavy black skillet on the stove, fry a mess of eggs in butter, layer bermuda onion slices and mayonnaise on bread, and slide the eggs aboard to made hearty sandwiches. She would put the sandwiches in a sack and tie it to the belt loops on one hip, then place three cold beers in a plastic bag and lash it to the opposite hip. Then she'd select a sharpened cane from the collection in her closet, flip the Closed sign on the front door of the pool hall, and head for the dense thickets and muckish terrain where snakes abounded, slithering and hissing, just asking for it.

As she fried the eggs on this Sunday morning, her birthday, Monique stood before the stove, her long gray hair down, not yet braided, brushing against her ankles, and stole looks at the rollabed in the pantry where Etta lay, the girl already awake, but feigning sleep.

"You about awake?" she asked gruffly.

The girl kept her eyes shut and breathed steadily in a fair imitation of true sleep.

"Get up," Monique said. She was stout, sturdy, and her brown eyes were large behind the lenses of horn-rimmed glasses. "These eggs are practically done."

The girl's eyes fluttered, and she sort of tossed on the bed, as if only now nearing consciousness.

"I raised three boys," Monique said, "and all of 'em was better fakers than that. Get on up, Etta."

"What time is it?" Etta asked, almost sourly.

"Time to get up and kill a snake, girl."

"What did you say?"

"I said it's snake killin' day, girl, and I'm up for it. Want to tag along?"

"Criminentlies," Etta said. She spun off the bed and began to dress.

"Wear old clothes," Monique said. "It'll be muddy from the overnight rain."

"I only got these clothes, m'am."

"Wear 'em, then. And I told you to call me Ma."

When the girl had come to the door during the night, Monique had turned on the front door light, looked at the girl standing on the stoop with a pink suitcase held to her chest, and known who she was before they even spoke. She'd given the girl milk with banana bread and butter to calm her, for she was fidgety and shyly evasive. They'd sat at the table and talked in sentence fragments for a half hour, then turned in. Monique had gone to bed thinking, she looks like a Shade, like a Shade girl, which is what I wanted, but never had.

The sandwiches made, Monique sat on a chair and began to braid the witchy length of her gray hair, braiding the strands into coils that she pinned up like a crown. Bright morning sun blared in through the small east window, shining on her back. A long black cigarette dangled from her lips.

Etta came into the kitchen, sniffed the sandwiches, then slouched against a wall.

"Do you really kill snakes?"

"Yup."

"You ain't shittin' me, are you?"

"I see John X. has passed his potty mouth on to you, girl."

"He says words like that are part of our language."

"Your dad says more ridiculous shit than any three lunatics do."

"Maybe. Sometimes he's right."

Monique began to pin the final braid into place.

"It's only fair to admit that, I s'pose." She stood and opened the closet door. "Look here."

On the inside of the door snakeskins were nailed to the wood and hung down like pennants, rustling as the door yawned wider.

"Wow!" Etta said. She advanced on the door, slowly approaching the slightly swaying snakeskins. She carefully raised her hands and began to feel the skins, and as the initial sensation was pleasant, she ran her fingers up the long dry length of the various copperheads, cottonmouths, and one stray rattlesnake. She leaned into the skins and smelled them. There were over a dozen faded, vanquished serpents nailed to the door, and the smell of them was neutral, but their colors and designs were exotic, fetching, and she pulled them to her face and pressed her young unpainted lips to the brittle, brilliant scales. "Ma—you killed *all* these?"

"Yup."

"They're so pretty—are they poisonous?"

Monique blew a cloud of smoke from the side of her mouth.

"The poisonous ones are *always* the prettiest."

"Gee, that's too bad."

"I s'pose, but it's something good to know."

The back screendoor squeaked as it was jerked open, and Nicole Webb walked into the kitchen, wearing a black T-shirt, washed-out bib overalls, and high-top sneakers. Her expression was vague, not quite awake, and her dark hair was amok.

"Coffee," she said. She had taken a chair at the table before she became aware of Etta. "Who're you?"

"Nic," Monique said, "this is Etta—Rene's half sister."

"I was gonna guess that," Nicole said. "How're you, Etta?"

"Peachy," Etta said. "You're Rene's girl?"

"That's right," said Monique.

"Approximately," Nicole said. "Where is he, anyhow?"

"Still asleep."

"Good."

Monique lashed the necessary bags to her belt, then

pulled three long sharp canes from the closet. She passed the canes out, keeping her favorite, a cracked pool cue that had been converted to a snaking instrument. She put a straw hat over the crown of her hair, cupped a hand to her ear, cocked her head, and said, "Can you hear 'em, girls? Their forked tongues are callin' me."

North along the railroad tracks the steady thump of Monique's heavy boots set the pace. Church bells were tolling in the far distance, the clanging bells causing the winos and bums who flopped beside the tracks in boxes and upturned rowboats and other makeshift suites to come awake. The derelicts pissed in the weeds or vomited or picked up nearly empty jugs for an eye-opener. The three generations of womanhood kept marching, stomping along to the pace set by the oldest among them, tapping their canes to the railroad ties in rhythm with their steps.

When the snakers were abreast of a slough, a slough in the midst of a foul but alluring thicket, the thicket rich in serpent potential, Monique turned off the tracks and down a slender path. Horseweed grew beside the path, taller than the tallest head among them, and though the weeds were beginning their autumnal wilt, they blocked from view any step but the next step. Nearly bare cottonwoods towered overhead, while limbs of the more squatty chinaberry, catalpa, and unknowns closed in snugly around the path. The path was clear but muddy, and the wet earth seemed to suck at footsteps.

After leaping over a small felled tree that had splayed across the path, Monique halted. She jabbed the sharp

point of her pole into the mud, her eyes surveying the lush
thicket, the fallen leaves and limbs and ancient muck of the
swamp.

"It's fall," she said, "and they could be in their holes.
Or this warm weather could have them out still—sunnin'
on rocks, lyin' in wait—let's beat 'em into the open, girls."

"It's *your* birthday, Ma," Nicole said. "Hope we find
you a present."

The snakers, their sharp tips down, began to poke into
dark corners, tangled vines, mysterious holes, jabbing with
their canes, driving the bladed tips into likely spots. They
snaked roughly parallel to the river. They swung their
poles, slashing through vines and under bushes, cracking
weak branches, sweating, joking, cursing, thoroughly en-
joying the hunt, eyes alert for anything poisonous that
might slither into view.

"Have you killed any?" whispered Etta to Nicole.

"Not really. Ma's skinned quite a few."

"Seventeen," Etta said. "I counted."

As they went deeper into the swamp they splashed
through shallow water and soft marsh mud. Grime clung
up to their hips. Eerie cypress grew in these wetlands, their
trunks swollen, and fluted. In the shallows cypress knees,
some a few inches in size, some several feet tall, rose above
the water, each supported by a vast root system, root sys-
tems that frequently tripped the snaking women. Every few
slashes of the canes seemed to occasion unseen plops into
water—a bull frog, perhaps, or a water turtle, or muskrat,
or maybe a cottonmouth as thick as a grown man's arm.

Near a cypress knee, gnarled and indomitable, Monique stood alongside Nicole, and lit a smoke.

"How're you feeling?" she asked. "Any mornin' sick-
ness?"

"Sort of," Nicole said. "More like constant confusion."

"Uh-huh. Yup. Girl, all I can say to you is—don't count on *him* to know what's right."

"The trouble is I don't trust *me* that much either," Nicole said. "I'm not exactly sittin' on top of the world."

Etta was spearing the thicket ahead, and Monique started to follow, but after two wet steps she called over her shoulder, "Sure you are."

After two more snakeless hours the women were hungry and thirsty but had seen only a single black milk snake, already dead and partly consumed.

Monique pried the tip of her pole under the snake and flipped it into the brush.

"Not much of a present," she said. "I think we should eat."

Monique led the way down the path to the river's edge. A huge white rock dike protruded into the wide flow, and the snakers picked their way out onto it. Mud covered them to the waist, their arms, necks, and cheeks splattered with dark swamp muck. Monique and Nicole, knowing the rituals, stood on white rocks and undressed, peeling down to their damp skivvies. Etta watched with suspicion for a moment, then did the same. The women squatted at the water's edge and rinsed the mud from their various shirts and pants and socks and overalls, then spread the clothes on rocks to dry in the sunlight.

"I believe a beer would refresh," Monique said, her eyes shadowed beneath the rim of her frayed straw hat.

Then the three snakers, clad only in underpants, their bodies open to the air, squatted on rocks, unwrapped the bags, and began to picnic.

Monique passed a beer to Nicole, then, after a brief

hesitation, passed one to Etta. Nicole popped the top and chugged.

"I'm definitely drinking," she said.

"I hear that."

When Etta popped the top on her brew, foam flew out. She licked the suds from the rim on the can, her eyes shining, licking carefully, coolly, as if she'd done this before.

The egg and onion sandwiches were distributed, and the women sat there, lunching beside the river, looking like a nude illustration of three crucial stages in a woman's life.

Etta ate her sandwich with big bites, her eyes straying to Nicole's interesting armpits, so full of hair, and Ma's huge heavy breasts that drooped toward the roll of fat around her belly.

"My mom has terrific knockers," Etta said. "Does that mean I'll have 'em like that, too?"

Nicole laughed, looking at her own smallish breasts.

"Don't ask me."

"Maybe," Monique said. She took her glasses off and wiped the lenses on her skivvies. "I'll bet *he* was fond of 'em."

"Huh?" Etta said. "I don't want 'em—they get in the way for sports. Mom couldn't even throw a baseball without makin' a face."

The noon bells at St. Peter's sounded, ringing faintly through the warm air.

"Why'd your daddy send you to me?" Monique asked.

"I can't talk about that."

"He told you that?"

"No. I just don't *know* why. That's why I can't talk about it."

"Was he drunk?"

"Well, just the normal."

"Mm-hmm."

Half of Etta's beer was gone, and she was buzzed, her eyes suddenly fluttering.

"You ever wondered what would've happened if they hadn't killed Christ for our sins?" she asked. "I mean, if instead they'd just dragged Him out back and slapped Him around some?"

Nicole and Monique raised up from their private thoughts and looked at her steadily.

Nicole said, "Now that is a morbid thing for a girl your age to say."

Monique grunted amiably. "She *ain't* sayin' it—that's Johnny Shade talkin'."

A cool peal of laughter came from Etta. She tapped a finger to her temple. "I got him memorized," she said.

"I better take some of that," Nicole said, and took the beer from the girl. She swished the beer in her mouth and swallowed. "My tummy is dry."

Monique nodded and said, "I think maybe you've made your mind up."

With the sandwiches eaten and the beers drunk, the snakers lay back on the rocks and silently sunned. After a while Etta sat up and said, "Hey! A tugboat!" The women came upright. "There's a man on deck lookin' at us!"

Nicole shaded her eyes with a flat hand.

"Oh," she said, "he's a little bit cute."

She stood, watching the man on the tug, and stretched her arms overhead.

*"Nicole!"* Etta said, "he'll—"

Then Monique stood beside Nicole, and, as the tug drew near, they turned their backs to the man on deck, bent over and rolled their undies to their ankles, shining contrasting moons across the river.

"Criminentlies!"

The man on deck called out something cheerful. Then another man rushed out to join him. They both waved frantically, and did flagrant pelvis bumps.

"Fuck you, too," Monique hissed under her breath. "Monkeys."

The tug whistled twice as it pulled away downstream.

Etta jumped up, now, and offered her own tiny hairless moon for view. She was giddy, bent over with her head between her knees, her skimpies stretched from ankle to ankle.

"Can they see this? Can they see this from there?"

"Maybe," Monique said. The old woman laughed. "You're okay, li'l girl. You did swell on the hunt. I watched you. You've got all kinds of Shade qualities."

"This is fun."

Soon after the tug disappeared, the women dressed. They put the trash into the bags, lifted their poles, and walked on up the path toward home. They stuck to the trail through the thicket, no longer pausing to thrash for snakes. On the railroad tracks Monique put an arm around Etta's shoulders. She held her close, then rubbed the girl's hair.

"You're one of us," she said. "No matter what might happen, Etta, we'll do what we can for you."

The sun beat down, and overhead a small band of late migrating birds scurried south.

"I'll let *that* sink in," Etta said.

When they reached the back door of the pool hall Monique unlocked it, pushed it open, and the tired women went directly to the table and collapsed into chairs, their poles clattering to the floor.

Monique Blanqui Shade slumped in her chair, her chin low, eyes on the snakeskins draped from the open closet door. She sighed.

"No snakes today," she said.

# part iv

## Que sera and so on

15.

There had been a time in river country when the sky from delta to headwaters blackened into one solid thunderhead, then busted open, punishing the land with far too many inches of rain in short order, and the big river, swollen by the runoff from the heart of the country, jumped its banks and kept on jumping, forever changing the face of the downriver world. The flood was named for its year, 1927, and in its wake towns became sloughs, riches became forlorn memories, and whole families were washed to the Gulf, never to be found. The swamps were flushed by the surging water, and all who lived there were forced to seek the haven afforded by higher ground, where they huddled in Red Cross camps and met the world that existed outside their own.

This was the first peek at life beyond the swamp for

most of the refugees, and as the weeks in the camp went by many of them came to like what they saw. When the big river calmed and the swamp settled back to level, families that had known no life but the swampy decided that the allure of wild rice ranching and nutria trapping was overshadowed by the grand tales they'd swallowed of city life, a place where sugar-cured hams were free so long as you bought a potato, pigeons were fat and sleek and tasted like shrimp, cash was doled out twice a month, and there was an endless supply of liquid cheer and hoochy-koochy bonhomie. The flood pushed these folks from the remote life of the swamp and into the bullshit embrace of the bluff, winking city.

John X. looked out the dusty bathroom window of Tip's place to the brown river wending its endless path through the night. He wedged his elbow against the sill to hold himself steady, then finished off the whisky in his glass. Among the families forced to flee before the flood were the Blanquis, who fled from a place with no name, deep in the swamp. They'd come to town in the summer of '27, three months after the flood, and it was because of that rushing water that he had, later on, met a certain fourteen-year-old Blanqui girl, whom he'd wooed with spontaneous ditties on the subject of his desire, and ended up married to. And though that terrible flood had killed his mother, her drowned body never recovered, it had also round about brought him a wife and progeny.

John X. leaned back from the window, and when he turned he saw a drunken face in the mirror over the sink and sadly realized that drunken face was his own. Criminentlies, he hadn't had his little angel to pour his whisky today, and on his own he'd made a mess. His little angel knew just the right size that an angel of whisky should be. On his own he had this problem with portions, and he'd been drunk since shortly after he'd come to on the couch at noon. His pale grizzled face was a blur in the mirror.

He looked blurrily at the blurred image of himself, and decided to shave. He opened the cabinet and found Tip's razor and shaving cream. The foam hissed into his palm, and John X. lathered it to his cheeks. He leaned closer to the light, then dropped his jaw and pulled the razor down as it cleared a wobbly path from his cheekbone. Two red dots of blood bloomed immediately. He was trying to be at Monique's for a seven-thirty dinner, but he'd seen the damn clock from a screwy angle and been thrown off on his reading. Two hours off. He'd believed it to be a quarter of six, which left plenty of time, only to look again in ten minutes and find that it was nearly eight, and he had to hurry. He flattened his lips and drew the razor rapidly over the bump of his chin. When he finished, thin furrows of whiskers that the razor had missed bristled up, and tiny bits of reddening toilet paper hung from the nicks he'd made on his skin.

He dressed in the front room. He selected the handsomest threads from his suitcase of dead man's finery. He struggled with the buttons, but overcame this new test of his dexterity. Unfortunately black sneakers were his only shoes, and he bent down to tie them. When he raised up, Lunch Pumphrey was standing in the doorway, all in black, his hat brim pulled down, one little hand stuffed in the pockets of his Levi's, the other little hand holding a Colt .45.

"Paw-Paw, I've had Enoch's orange truck staked out for hours," Lunch said agreeably. "I got tired of waitin' for you to show yourself."

"Hey, sorry about that Lunch—" John X. said. "Say, what'cha drinkin'?"

"Oh my head's still poundin' from last night, Paw-Paw. I don't think I want to drink none."

John X. straightened the collar on his shirt and stood up straight, sneaking a glance toward the couch where Enoch's pistol was hidden. "I'm gonna guess pain is in the forecast for me, huh, Lunch?"

"You don't gotta guess, Paw-Paw."

"Well," John X. said, "that forecast calls for a drink." He lurched across the room toward the kitchen and his bottle of Maker's Mark. "I guess I half figured you'd be showin' up."

"You know I'm relentless this way," Lunch said.

John X. pulled the cork with a flourish, and took a deep sniff of the sweet sour mash, then raised the bottle neck and drank deeply.

"Where's the money?" Lunch asked.

"Oh, hell, slick, all that's left of that money is a *beautiful* memory, and nine hundred bucks. I had myself a time blowin' it," John X. said, shaking his head. "Yeah, Lunch, it all went to good causes, if you call bookies good causes. I'm gonna guess you don't."

John X.'s wrinkled face took on the mobile features of an animated raconteur, and he waved his arms with a sloppy charm.

"Looky here, Paw-Paw, you're sayin' nine hundred bucks is all you got left from forty-seven thousand dollars?"

"Well, really, nine hundred and fifty," John X. said, waving his bottle around. "But I'd like to keep a fifty so's I could slip it to ol' St. Pete—it might make the difference."

Lunch Pumphrey's dark, sepulchral eyes narrowed, and he eased his snap-brim hat back from his face.

"What you did to me proves you're in-sane. I might as well hear the details."

"Randi was furious with me, and at Pascagoula she jumped out with the kid and split. So, bein' alone, I decided I'd take that money of yours and run it up to where I was a millionaire!" He shook a cigarette loose, then flipped his eight-ball lighter open, and lit it.

"See, I took the advice of the pigskin experts, Lunch, and I put fifteen K down on them wily 'Bama boys. Saturday last, they lined up against a team from Florida whose star quarterback and favorite wide receiver had just been carted off to jail on rape charges. That oughta be an edge, right? Short of a fuckin' jailbreak that game *had* to be a lock for the Crimson Tide. But as you might know, late in the fourth quarter their stud runnin' back, the one that beat that burglary rap back in the spring, coughed it up inside the Florida ten-yard line, and that Florida linebacker who'd just come off suspension from that summertime assault beef the papers were full of, jumped on the ball and kept 'Bama from coverin' the spread."

John X. sucked on a cigarette, shook his head, and said, "Makes you wanta puke, don't it?" The old man looked at Lunch's face and grimaced. "Criminentlies, that's what I did to your face, huh? Nothin' broke?"

Lunch leaned against the wall, tapping the barrel of the pistol to his thigh.

"Just a bruise," he said. "Some pain."

"Randi told me I'd fucked up bad."

"Randi's a smart chick," Lunch said. "So where's the other thirty-two grand?"

"Oh, Slick," John X. said. "It gets worse." He flapped his elbows and gestured to the sky. "I doubled up to get the money back."

"Shit, that's stupid," Lunch said. "That's the same way I lost it to Short Paul in the first place."

"But that's what happened," John X. said. "I mean, can you believe Notre Dame could get beat by the Air Force Academy?"

"That was a shocker," Lunch said.

"Course then I spent another grand or so eatin' and drinkin', you know. I like good whisky."

"Good whisky an' bad luck, looks like to me," Lunch said. "You know I'm gonna kill you, don't you?"

A cigarette in one hand, a bottle of Maker's Mark in the other, John X raised his arms wide over his head.

"Que sera and so on."

"Gimme what you got," Lunch said. "And forget holdin' out that last fifty."

John X. pulled the roll of greenbacks from his pocket. He swayed loosely as he leaned toward Lunch, and handed him the wad.

"I hope you had fun," Lunch said, "cause your fun is over."

"I know," John X. said. "I should be halfway to Dallas by now."

Lunch briskly tapped down the brim of his little black hat, then pointed the pistol out the door.

"Let's take a little ride in my Bug," he said.

"Sure," John X. said, lifting his bottle expansively. "Feelin' the call of the open road, huh? That's always been my downfall, too, Lunch."

There were a handful of flowers he'd pulled out of a neighbor's yard resting on the kitchen table, and as John X.

passed, he paused to break a blossom off and insert it in his lapel. "I don't know what these are," he said. "Do you?"

"Might be tulips," Lunch said.

They crossed the wooden deck, their footsteps echoing out across the water, then down the slab steps to the gravel drive. Gravel crunched underfoot as they walked to Lunch's VW which was parked discreetly at the end of the drive. John X. took a deep breath of the autumn night air, then looked up at the bowl of stars above his head. Lunch's pistol prodded him in the back when they reached the VW.

"Open the trunk," Lunch said.

John X. pushed the button in and raised the bonnet, the hinges groaning loudly in the silent night. He looked down at three huge rocks on the bottom of the trunk.

"What are the rocks for?" John X. asked.

"Now, don't you worry about them, Paw-Paw." Lunch raised his pistol and planted it squarely at the back of John X.'s head. "Get in."

The old man crawled inside, and curled into a fetal position on top of the rocks. He looked up at Lunch.

"Look all around you, Paw-Paw. Notice *every* little thing. Appreciate it all at once—and say good-bye."


The birthday party was haunted by a white plate that set empty on the table. Monique Blanqui Shade hunched in her chair, smoking a long black cigarette. She wore a flower above her ear, a dainty gesture Etta had talked her into, and now she pulled the yellow rose from her hair and tossed it beside a dirty plate. Dinner had been eaten, and a jug of red wine was being passed around. All the children were gathered here. Rene and Nicole were avoiding eye contact, pointedly not talking to each other beyond banal courtesies, Nicole topping her wine glass with every passing of the jug. Big Tip, lonely since Gretel had been grounded by Mrs. Carter, shoveled in cake and smiled regularly; Francois, with his sports coat elegantly hung from the chair back, sat with his wife, Charlotte, a blonde of robust physique who smiled a lot, but always shrewdly studied the family as if her visits were part of a sociological inquiry. She'd expressed the keenest interest in meeting John X. Shade.

"He's halfway to Dallas by now," Etta said, looking at the empty plate. She propped her chin in her hand. "Mom predicted this."

"I don't care," Francois said. "He was *always* a phantom to me."

"Can I play pool with his cue now, Ma?" Etta asked.

Monique Blanqui Shade raised one long gray eyebrow, then gazed at Tip.

Tip shrugged, took a sip of wine. "Why not? I brought it back for him. Try it out, kid. Sure. Why not use the best? It's how he liked to do."

Etta got up from the table and went to the adjoining room where a pool table sat under a hanging lamp. She unlatched her father's black cue case, then lifted the sleek Balabushka from the slots lined with green felt. Then Rene was at her side.

"Pretty, ain't it?" Rene said. "Here, let me show you how the pros do it." He took the two pieces from her, then screwed the halves together. Rene picked up a square of chalk from the table edge and rapidly buffed the cue tip. "That's how to chalk the cue," he said. "Chalk between each shot. Always." He slid the Balabushka appreciatively through his fingers, and leaned over to break. He smacked the cue ball low and drove it into the rack, spreading the balls around the table. "Yeah, Ol' Johnny won hisself a lot of dough and free drinks with this piece of wood, kid."

"Grampa Enoch told me Dad was real good once."

"He sure was, kid," Rene said. "Course you spend fifty years at this game you *oughta* get pretty good."

Etta looked up at her half brother, twisting the crucifix in her ear. "He said his eyes got bad."

"He used to have good eyes," Rene said, "and a steady hand and the nerve of a back-door man."

Rene handed Etta the Balabushka cue. She leaned over the pool table. "He never let me touch it before," she said.

The party was breaking down along gender lines, Nicole and Charlotte remaining at the table with Monique— Nicole swirling the red wine in her glass, but looking deflated somehow; Charlotte saying, "What a lovely time this is," but looking at her gold wristwatch; Monique sitting there, her eyes unfocused, her attention somewhere else. A couple of birthday presents lay opened on the table—a teapot in the shape of a fish, a green silk blouse, one used bass lure.

From time to time there was a loud clacking of balls on the pool table.

Rene, Tip, and Francois congregated over at the window, looking out at Lafitte, the dark cobblestoned street they'd spent their youths on and never left far behind.

"I guess I believed him this time," Tip said.

"Sucker," Francois said.

"But that was before I knew he had nine hundred bucks."

The three sons stood in a rank, looking onto the black

empty street, and finally Rene cupped a hand to his ear and said, "You hear it?"

Tip nodded slowly and said, "Honk, honk—"

Then, recognizing the prelude, all three sons hoisted the glasses in their hands together, raised them in salute toward the dark street as if seeing a certain bullet-shaped '51 Ford cruising their way, and said in unison, "Hey, assholes."